FATELESS

Imre Kertész

FATELESS

TRANSLATED BY

Christopher C. Wilson and Katharina M. Wilson

NORTHWESTERN UNIVERSITY PRESS
Evanston, Illinois

Hydra Books
Northwestern University Press
Evanston, Illinois 60208-4210

Originally published in Hungarian under the title *Sorstalanság*
by Szépirodalmi Könyvkiadó. Copyright © 1975 by Imre
Kertész. English translation copyright © 1992 by Northwestern
University Press. Published 1992. All rights reserved.

This translation has been funded in part by the National
Endowment for the Arts.

10 9 8 7 6 5 4 3

Printed in the United States of America

ISBN 0-8101-1024-5 (cloth)
ISBN 0-8101-1049-0 (paper)

Library of Congress Cataloging-in-Publication Data

Kertész, Imre, 1929–
    [Sorstalanság. English]
    Fateless / Imre Kertész ; translated by Christopher C. Wilson
and Katharina M. Wilson.
        p. cm.
    ISBN 0-8101-1024-5 (alk. paper).—ISBN 0-8101-1049-0
(pbk. : alk. paper)
    1. Holocaust, Jewish (1939–1945)—Fiction. I. Title.
PH3281.K3815S6713 1992
894'.51133—dc20   92-16930
                                                          CIP

Translators' Acknowledgments

We would like to acknowledge our gratitude to Imre Kertész for his invaluable help during the preparation of the manuscript, to the Soros Foundation for enabling us to travel to Hungary to work with the author, and to Dr. James Wilhelm for his insightful editorial comments.

Fateless

1

Today I skipped school. That is, I went, but only to ask my teacher to excuse me from class. I gave him my father's letter asking if I could be excused for "personal reasons." My teacher wanted to know the reasons. I told him my father was being conscripted into the labor service. That ended any further objection.

I hurried toward our shop—not home. Father had said, "That's where they'll be expecting me." He also added that I should hurry because I might be needed there. Actually that was why he had asked that I should be excused from school. Or maybe he wanted me near him on this, his last day before he was going to be torn away from home. For he did say this, although admittedly on another occasion. If I recall correctly, he had mentioned it to Mother when he called her this morning. For today, you see, is Thursday, and on Thursdays and Sundays my afternoons technically belong to her. But my father had told her: "It is beyond my power to let George visit you today," and then he gave her the above-mentioned reason. But then again, maybe he didn't. I was a little sleepy this morning because of the air raid last night, and it's possible I don't recall the conversation correctly. But I am absolutely certain he spoke those words, if not to Mother then to someone else. I also spoke briefly with her; I no longer remember exactly what I said. I suppose she was a little miffed because I had to be brief with her since my father was also there. But after all, today I have to please him.

When I was almost ready to leave home, my stepmother addressed a few private words to me while we were standing in the foyer. She said she hoped that "on this our dark, dark day," she could "count on my good behavior." I was at a loss for an answer, and so I remained silent. But she misunderstood my silence, for she continued by suggesting she hadn't intended to question my sensitivity. That, she knew, was superfluous, for she had no doubt that I, now in my fifteenth year and a grown-up boy, could fully grasp the weight of the blow that had fallen upon us. This was her phrasing. I nodded. I saw that this satisfied her. Her hands even moved in my direction, and I was almost afraid she was thinking of hugging me. But that didn't happen; she only sighed deeply, letting out a long, trembling breath. I noticed that her eyes were misting over. It was embarrassing. Then I was given permission to go.

I walked from school to our shop. It was a clear and warm morning, considering that it was early spring. I began to unbutton my coat, but then I reconsidered. In the light breeze my coat flaps could be tossed back to hide my yellow star, which was going against the regulations. In certain ways I had to handle myself more circumspectly now.

Our lumber store is a cellar on one of the nearby side streets. Steep steps go down into the darkness. I found my father and my stepmother in the office—a narrow glass cage lighted like an aquarium, right at the foot of the steps. Mr. Suto was there with them. I knew him from when we employed him as a bookkeeper and as the manager of our other open-air lumberyard, which he had later bought from us. At any rate, that's the way we refer to it: for racially speaking Mr. Suto was all okay; he wasn't forced to wear a yellow star, so the whole arrangement was simply one of those business transactions that, if I understand correctly, was just meant to help him keep an eye out for our profit and also to prevent us from having to lose all our income from the yard.

I greeted him somewhat differently from in the past, because, in a sense, his fortune had now risen above ours. My father and my stepmother now listened more carefully to him.

He, on the other hand, was all the more insistent on addressing my father as "sir" and my stepmother as "dear lady," as if nothing at all had happened. He also never forgot to kiss her hand. Well, he received me in his usual teasing manner. He didn't pay any attention to my yellow star. I stood where I was, right next to the door, and they kept talking about whatever my arrival had interrupted. My own hunch was that I had disturbed some sort of serious discussion. At first I couldn't understand what they were talking about. For a second I even shut my eyes tight because they were a little blurred from the sunlight outside. But then Father said something surprising that made me open my eyes wide. Everywhere on Mr. Suto's brownish, round face, with his thin, tiny mustache and the gap between his two white front teeth, yellow-purple sun splotches jumped around like boils.

The next sentence was spoken by my father. He mentioned some kind of "merchandise" that "it would be best if Mr. Suto carried off with him immediately." Mr. Suto raised no objection, so Father removed from his desk a little parcel that was wrapped in tissue paper and bound with strings. Only then did I see the type of merchandise they had been talking about, because I immediately recognized the package by its flat form: it held a box. The box, in turn, held our finest jewelry and other valuables. In fact, I believe that it was precisely for my sake that they referred to it as merchandise, so I wouldn't recognize it. Mr. Suto quickly buried it in his bag. Then a little argument developed between them. Mr. Suto pulled out a pen and insisted above all on giving my father a receipt for the goods. He kept insisting, although Father told him not to be "childish," that there was no need for such formalities between them. I noticed that this made Mr. Suto feel quite good. He then said, "I know that you trust me, sir, but in practical life everything has to have some order and form." He even involved my stepmother: "Am I not right, dear lady?" But she, with a tired smile on her lips, mumbled something about leaving this matter entirely to the gentlemen.

All this was beginning to bore me, when Mr. Suto finally

replaced his pen. Then they started talking about the question of storage: What was to be done with all the wood here? Father was for speeding things up before the authorities "put their paws on the goods." He asked Mr. Suto, with his business experience and expertise, to help my stepmother do this. Mr. Suto, turning to her, immediately declared: "That goes without saying, dear lady. After all, we shall be in constant contact because of all the accounting details." I think he was referring to our other lumberyard. After what seemed like an eternity, he began to leave. With his face clouded over, he shook my father's hand for some time; he felt that "in such moments no place exists for long speeches," and so he only wished to offer one parting word to him, namely, "See you as soon as possible, sir." My father answered him with a little half smile: "Let's hope so, Mr. Suto." At the same time my stepmother opened her handbag, removed a handkerchief, and put it to her eyes. Some strange sounds were welling up inside her throat. There was silence. The situation was very embarrassing, and I felt that I too should do something. But everything was happening so quickly I couldn't think of anything intelligent to do.

I saw Mr. Suto also becoming uncomfortable. "My dear lady," he said, "you really shouldn't. Really." He looked a little frightened. He bowed down and almost dropped his lips onto my stepmother's hand, as if to give her the usual hand-kiss. Then he bolted for the door. I barely had enough time to jump out of his way. He even forgot to tell me good-bye. Even after he disappeared, we could hear the sound of his heavy steps resounding on the wooden stairs.

After a few moments of silence, my father said, "Well, that's one load off our backs." Then my stepmother, with a still somewhat controlled voice, asked if my father should not, after all, have accepted that written receipt from Mr. Suto. But he answered that such a receipt was totally devoid of any practical value. Furthermore, he added, trying to hide it would be more dangerous than trying to hide the very box itself. And he finished by telling her that now "we have to put all our eggs in one basket, that is, we have to rely on Mr. Suto with absolute faith, especially since right now no other solution is available to us anyway." After this explanation my stepmother became quiet, but she did reply that although my father was probably right, she would still have somehow felt more secure with a receipt in her hand, although she couldn't explain exactly why. Then my father urged her to begin the work awaiting them, because, as he said, "time is flying." He wanted to give her the books so she could manage them without his being around and so the business wouldn't have to come to a halt because he was being held in a labor camp. Meanwhile, he also spoke with me briefly. He asked me if they had allowed me to miss school without raising a ruckus, and so on. Finally he instructed me to sit down and be quiet until he and my stepmother finished poring over the books.

The trouble was that this took forever. For a while I tried being patient, thinking of my father or, more precisely, that he would be leaving tomorrow and that I probably wouldn't be seeing him for a long, long time. But after some more time had elapsed, I became worn out by these thoughts, and then, since I could do nothing else for my father, I became bored. Sitting around wore me down, and so, just to do something, I got up and went over to the spigot to get a drink. They said nothing. Later I went out back between the rows of lumber to urinate. I washed my hands at the rusty tiled sink when I returned. Then I opened my school bag, took out my snack, and ate it; to finish it off, I drank some more water from the spigot. They still said nothing, and so I sat back down at my appointed place. Then I became terrifically bored, and for a long time.

It was already midday when we went back out into the street. My eyes were blurred again. This time the light bothered them. My father kept fumbling with the locks of the two gray iron padlocks. He seemed to be doing this almost on purpose. Then he gave my stepmother the keys, since he no longer had any need of them. I knew this because he told me so. My stepmother opened her handbag. I feared she was again searching for her handkerchief, but she only put the keys there. Then we rushed along. At first I thought we were going back home, but no, our first stop was at a shop. My stepmother had a long list of Father's needs for the labor camp. She had already bought some of the items yesterday, but we had to track down the others today.

Walking along, with all three of us wearing yellow stars, was awkward. When I'm alone, I'm rather amused by the stars, but with them I felt some tension. I can't explain why. Later I stopped paying attention to the stars entirely. The stores were all crowded with people, except for the one where we bought the knapsack. There we were the only customers. The air was thick with the sickening smell of prepared linen. The shop-keeper—a yellowed, tiny old man with glittering false teeth and with elbow pads on his arms—and his fat wife were very cordial to us. They piled all kinds of goods on the countertop directly in front of us. I noticed that the shopkeeper addressed the old woman as "my child" and had her chase down each and every item. I knew this shop, by the way, because it was near home, but I'd never entered it before. Actually it was a kind of sporting goods store, but they also sold many other items. Recently they had started stocking some homemade yellow stars, because, of course, yellow cloth was scarce (my step-mother took care to buy what we needed long ago). Unless I'm mistaken, they had invented the idea of stretching the cloth over a piece of cardboard. And so, the star was, naturally, more attractive; the rays were not ridiculously jagged, as they were on some amateurish ones. I noticed that their own chests were decorated with their products, as if they were wearing the stars to encourage customers to buy some.

The old woman returned with all the goods. Before that, though, the shopkeeper asked, "Might I be permitted to ask if perhaps you are shopping for labor camp service?" My step-mother said yes. The old man nodded sadly. He even lifted his two gaunt, liver-spotted hands and with a sympathetic move-ment dropped them down in front of himself on the counter-top. Then my stepmother mentioned that we also needed a knapsack and asked if he had any. The old man hesitated, then said, "For you, yes." He called over to his wife, "Child, bring one out of storage for the gentleman." The knapsack was perfect. The shopkeeper had his wife bring out a few other items that, he thought, Father "cannot do without where he is going." Generally he spoke very sensitively and sympathetically to us, and whenever possible he avoided the use of the term *labor camp*.

He showed us all kinds of useful items—a hermetically sealed food container, a pocketknife with several tools inside, a side pouch, and so on—items that, as he noted, people under similar circumstances always wanted from him. My stepmother bought the pocketknife. I also liked it. Then when we had bought what we needed, the shopkeeper called to his wife, "Cash register!" With great difficulty the old woman wedged her plump body, which was stuffed into a black dress, in between the cash register and an upholstered armchair. The shopkeeper walked us all the way to the door. There he let us know that he hoped to have the good fortune to serve us again, and then, leaning over, he whispered to my father, "In the way we hope, sir, you and I."

Now, indeed, we were finally returning home. We lived in a large rental apartment building near the square, where there was also a streetcar stop. We had already climbed to the first floor when my stepmother remembered that she had forgotten to exchange her bread stamps. So I had to go back to the baker. I got into the shop only after milling around outside for a while.

First I was waited on by the baker's blond, large-breasted wife. She was the one who snipped off the appropriate square from the bread coupon. Then the baker weighed the bread. He didn't respond to my greeting. It was common knowledge in the neighborhood that he couldn't stand Jews. That's why he tossed me a piece of bread a few grams short of the allotment. But I heard some talk that this was how he also kept some of the bread. And somehow, from his angry glance and his clever movements, I understood at that moment why he had no choice but to dislike Jews. For if he liked them, he'd be left with the unpleasant feeling that he was cheating them. This way he acted according to his convictions, his acts being governed by an ideal, and that made everything entirely different, of course.

I rushed home from the baker's because I was starved, and that was why I was willing to have only a word with Anne-Marie. Just as I was beginning to climb the stairs, she started hopping down. She lives on our floor with the Steiner family, whom we have lately been seeing at old man Fleischmann's every evening. In the past we took little notice of our neighbors, but now we are discovering that we are of the same genus, and that necessitates a brief exchange of ideas. The two of us usually talk about other things; that's how I discovered that Mr. and Mrs. Steiner are really only Anne-Marie's aunt and uncle. Since her parents are getting a divorce and they haven't yet been able to reach a settlement, they decided it would be better for her to stay here than with either of them. Before that she was in a private institution for the same reason I was in one. She is, like me, about fourteen years old. She has a long neck. Underneath her yellow star her chest is beginning to round out. She too was sent to the baker. She wanted to know if I wouldn't like playing a little gin rummy, the four of us, she and the two sisters who live on the floor directly above us. Anne-Marie keeps up her friendship with them, but I only know them in passing, from the hall and from the air raid shelter. The smaller sister looks to be only eleven or twelve years old, and the older, said Anne-Marie, is the same age as she. Sometimes when I happen to be in our room facing the courtyard, I see her comings and goings in the hallway, and a couple of times I met her down by the gate. I thought that this way I could get to know her better. That was what I wanted to do. But I immediately remembered my father, and I told Anne-Marie, "No, not today, because they've called up Father." Then she recalled that she had heard something at home from her uncle about my father's situation. So she answered, "Sure." We fell silent for a moment; then she asked, "How about tomorrow?" But I told her that the day after tomorrow would be better. And I quickly added, "Maybe."

When I got home I found my father and stepmother already seated at the table. While she was filling my plate, my stepmother asked, "Are you hungry?" I answered "ravenously" straight out, not thinking of anything else, because, after all, that was the case. So she piled some food on my plate, and she barely put anything on hers. My father noticed this and asked her why. She said something along the lines that at this particular time her stomach was unable to keep down any kind of food, and then I realized my mistake. My father, though, disagreed. His argument was that she shouldn't neglect herself, especially not now when her strength and stamina were most needed. My stepmother didn't respond, but I heard something, and when I looked up, I noticed what it was: she was crying. Again, this was very embarrassing. I tried looking down at my plate, but I still noticed my father's movement as he reached over for her hand. A minute later they were very, very quiet. When I carefully raised my eyes and looked at them, they were sitting holding hands, looking in a fixed way at each other, the way a man and a woman do. I never liked this, and even now it bothered me, although I guess it was a perfectly natural thing. I still didn't like it. Who knows why?

It was much better when they started talking again. The conversation turned to Mr. Suto briefly, and then to the box and to our other lumberyard. I heard my father saying he felt reassured that at least these were in good hands. My stepmother shared his confidence, although in passing she mentioned the receipt and the uncertainty, since everything was based on words of confidence alone, and she questioned whether that was sufficient. My father shrugged and replied, "There is no longer any certainty about anything, not only in business but in every other part of life." My stepmother immediately agreed, exhaling a deep sigh. She already regretted having voiced her concerns and begged my father not to dwell on such things. But then he began wondering how my stepmother would manage having to wrestle with such grave problems falling on her as they were during this heavy time, all alone and without him to help. My stepmother replied that she wouldn't be alone because, after all, I'd be by her side. We two, she continued, would care for each other until my father returned. And she asked, with her head turned and tilted slightly toward me, "Isn't that so?" She smiled, but her lips were trembling. I told her, "Yes, of course." My father looked at me too; his eyes were very gentle. That somehow got to me, and to do something for him, I pushed away my plate. He noticed and asked why I had pushed it away. I told him I had no appetite. I saw that he was touched; he stroked my head, and because of that touch, for the very first time this day, something constricted in my throat—not tears, but I felt some sort of queasiness. I wished that my father were already gone. It was a very bad wish, but I felt it so clearly that I couldn't think anything else about him, and I was all confused at that moment. Afterward, I could have cried, but I didn't have time for it because some guests were arriving.

My stepmother had mentioned them earlier. "Only the immediate family is coming," she said. And then she added, responding to some subtle gesture of Father's, "After all, they want to say good-bye to you. It's perfectly natural." At this point the bell was already ringing. My stepmother's sister and her mother came first. Shortly thereafter, my grandfather and grandmother also arrived. We quickly sat Grandmother on the couch because she can barely see, even though the lenses of her glasses are as thick as a magnifying glass, and she's at least as deaf. But she still wants to involve herself in everything and tries to make herself useful. So there was a lot of bother associated with her. For one thing, you constantly have to scream in her ear to explain a conversation, and also you have to arrange things so as to try to prevent her from taking part in whatever is going on, because it would only create chaos.

My stepmother's mother arrived wearing a pointed, warlike hat with a brim. A feather angled across the front. Soon, however, she removed it, and then you could see her beautiful thinning snow-white hair and her thinly braided small bun. She has a narrow yellow face and two large dark eyes. From her neck two withered leather folds of skin were hanging. She reminds you of a very intelligent, finely bred hound. Her head is always shaking a little bit. She was given the task of packing my father's knapsack, because she's the one who knows the most about these kinds of things. She set herself to the task at once, using the list that my stepmother gave her.

My stepmother's sister was of no use whatever. She is much older than my stepmother and also looks quite different, almost as if they weren't sisters. She is small and pudgy and has the face of a constantly amazed baby. She gabbed all the time; she cried too and embraced everyone. Only with much difficulty could I tear myself from her soft, powder-smelling breast. When she sat down, all her body's flesh cascaded over her short upper legs. And then to mention my grandfather: he stood next to Grandmother's couch and listened to her complaints with a patient, motionless face. At first she sobbed about Father's situation, but then this worry was supplanted by her own problems. She complained about her headache and the ringing and buzzing in her ears caused by her high blood pressure. My grandfather is used to this; he didn't even answer, but he didn't stir from her side. He stayed there until the end. I didn't hear him utter a single word or see him open his mouth one time, but every time I looked in that direction, I saw him in that same corner, slowly looking darker and darker as the afternoon progressed.

In addition, my stepmother's cousin arrived, together with her husband. I call him Uncle Vili. He has a slight physical defect; that's why he wears one shoe with a thicker sole than the other, and it is also the reason why he can thank his lucky stars for his being excused from labor camp duty. His face is pear-shaped, wide, bold, rounded on top, and thinner around his cheeks and toward his neck. His opinion is respected in the family because before he opened a betting office, he was in the newspaper business. Now, too, he wanted to inform us about some interesting news that he had from "reliable sources" and that he called "absolutely trustworthy." He sat down in an armchair, and stretching out his bad leg and rubbing his hands together with a dry noise, he informed us that "very soon a fundamental change is to be expected in our situation," because "secret negotiations" have begun concerning us "between the Germans and the Allied Forces, at the mediation of neutral powers." The Germans, Uncle Vili explained, "have themselves recognized the hopelessness of their position at the front." It was his opinion that we, the "Budapest Jewry," could act as bargaining chips in their efforts to squeeze some advantages from the Allied Forces at the price of our skins. The Allies, of course, would do everything possible in our favor. Here he mentioned an "important factor" that he knew from his newspaper experience, which he called "world opinion"; he said it was shaken up by what had happened to us. "The bargaining is, of course, tough," he continued, "and that is precisely the explanation for the momentary severity of the present orders against us. But all these are simply the natural results of the larger game in which we are the pawns of an international blackmail of gigantic proportions." He also said that he, who knew good and well what was going on "behind the scenes," considered this severity mostly just a "spectacular bluff" for the purpose of jacking up the price, and he was simply asking us for a little patience until "all the events unfold."

At this my father asked if all this was expected to happen tomorrow, and was he to consider his summons as mere bluff, and should he perhaps simply stay home tomorrow? Then Uncle Vili got a little tongue-tied and answered: "No, no, of course not." But he added that he for one was entirely at ease in his conviction that my father would return home soon. "We are in the twelfth hour," he said, rubbing his hands together constantly. And then he added: "I wish I had been this sure of some of my other tips. I wouldn't be a pauper now." He wanted to go on, but my stepmother and her mother had just finished packing the knapsack, and so my father got up to test its weight.

The last person to arrive was my stepmother's oldest brother, Uncle Lajos. He fills a very important honorary position in our family, though I can't tell exactly what it is. Right away he wanted to speak privately with my father. My impression was that this made my father nervous, and while very polite, he was determined to get it all over with quickly. Then, completely unexpectedly, Uncle Lajos cornered me. He said he wanted to "have a little chat with me." He dragged me over to a deserted corner of the room and stood me against a wardrobe facing him. He began by saying that I knew full well that my father was going to leave us tomorrow. I told him yes, I knew. Then he wanted to know if I would miss my father's presence. I answered, getting nervous about his question: "Yes, of course." And because I somehow thought this was not quite enough, I added right away: "Very much." As a response, he kept nodding his head with a plaintive look on his face.

But then I learned some interesting and surprising facts from him: for instance, that a portion of my life that he called "the carefree, happy years of childhood" had been brought to a close by today's sad events. Surely, he said, I thought of it this way. I admitted that I hadn't. But surely, he continued, his words didn't come as a total surprise to me. I repeated, "No, they don't." Then he informed me that, with my father's departure, my stepmother had no one to lean on, and even though the family "will keep an eye on us," still her chief support from now on would have to be me. Indeed, he said I would have to discover what "worry and sacrifice" meant well before my time, because obviously I wouldn't be as well off as before—and he didn't want to hide that from me, since we were now talking man to man. "Now," he said, "you too are part of the common Jewish fate." Then he elaborated on this, mentioning that this fate meant a "millennium of continuing persecutions" that Jews had had to accept "with acquiescence and self-sacrificing patience" because the punishment was doled out by God for the sins of our ancestors. For this reason He alone was the one from whom we could expect mercy. God, on the other hand, expected us to endure "everything according to our talents and abilities" in this grave situation that He had set out for us. I, for example, Uncle Lajos told me, would have to accept my role as head of the family. He asked me if I felt the strength and preparation necessary for the task. Even though I didn't understand his train of thought exactly—especially what he said about the sins of the Jews and their God—still I was gripped by his words. So I answered, "Yes, I do." He seemed content. "That's right," he said. He always knew that I was an intelligent boy who could "muster" deep emotions and who had "a serious sense of responsibility"; and he found some solace from that in the midst of so many tribulations. Then he raised my chin with his hairy fingers and moist palms and said in a quiet, somewhat trembling voice: "Your father is preparing himself for a long journey. Have you prayed for him?" There was some severity in his eyes, and that, perhaps, was the reason why a painful sense of omission with regard to my father welled up inside me, because, in fact, I wouldn't have thought of this on my own. But now, since he raised this subject with me, I immediately began to feel it like a burden, and so, in order to be free of it, I admitted: "No, I haven't." "Then come with me," he said.

I had to accompany him to the outer room facing the courtyard. There we prayed, surrounded by some old, unused pieces of furniture. First Uncle Lajos placed a round, silky little black cap on the back part of his head where there was a clearing bordered by his thinning gray hair. I too had to bring my hat in from the foyer. Then he removed both a bound black book with red sides and his glasses from the upper inside pocket of his coat. He started to recite a prayer, and I had to repeat after him as he read aloud. At first this went quite well, but soon I got a little tired of this work, and I was a little annoyed that I didn't understand a single word of what we were telling God, because He had to be addressed in Hebrew, and I don't speak that language. This way, all I could do in order to follow Uncle Lajos was to watch carefully the movement of his lips, so that the only memory of the event that remained was the spectacle of those wetly moving fleshy lips and the chaotic murmur of a foreign language that we mumbled to ourselves. I also remember another picture that I saw through the window above Uncle Lajos's shoulders: the older sister was hurrying home through the corridor opposite our flat. I think I got a little confused for a moment with the text. But still, at the end of the prayers, Uncle Lajos seemed content, from the expression on his face, and I almost felt it myself: indeed, we had accomplished something about my father's affairs. And really, finally, this was a lot better than that burdening, demanding feeling earlier.

We went back to the room facing the street. Dusk was coming on. We closed the windowpanes, which were covered by dark paper, shutting out a bluish, moist spring evening. In this way the room narrowed in on us. I was worn out by the talking. Also the smoke from the cigarettes started to irritate my eyes. I kept yawning. My stepmother's mother was sitting at the table. She had brought our dinner in a large bag. She had even gotten some meat on the black market. She had told us about it earlier, when she arrived. My father had paid her for it from his leather wallet. We were seated at dinner when suddenly Uncle Steiner and Uncle Fleischmann arrived. They too wanted to say good-bye to my father. Uncle Steiner began immediately by saying, "Please don't let us disturb you. My name is Steiner. Please don't get up." On his feet he was wearing worn slippers, his stomach bulged from his open waistcoat, and in his mouth was the eternal stinking remnant of a cigar. His head, large and red, contrasted strangely with his childlike hairdo: he wears his hair parted in the middle.

Standing next to him, Uncle Fleischmann was dwarfed, for he is small and carefully groomed, with white hair, grayish skin, and glasses like an owl's eyes; his face always shows a somewhat concerned expression. Wordlessly, at Uncle Steiner's side, he kept wringing his hands; it seemed to be his way of apologizing for Uncle Steiner. (Maybe I'm wrong. I can't be certain of this.) The two old men are inseparable, although they are constantly disagreeing; on no single issue do they see eye to eye. They both shook my father's hand, one right after the other. Uncle Steiner also slapped him on the back. He called Father "old boy" and cracked a stale joke: "Chin up, never give way to despair," he said, and Uncle Fleischmann nodded for emphasis. They said that they would keep looking after me and the "young lady" (as they called my stepmother). Uncle Steiner kept fluttering his eyelashes. Then he drew my father to his belly and gave him a bear hug. When they left, everything was drowned out by the clanking noise of the silver, the hum of conversation, the aromas from the food, and the impenetrable tobacco smoke. Through it all I could catch the disconnected image of an occasional face or movement. I especially recall the palsied, bony yellow head of my stepmother's mother as she attended to everyone's plate; Uncle Lajòs's hands extended outward in protest: no, he'd have none of the meat since it was pork and was not permitted by his faith; and the puffy cheeks of my stepmother's sister, her jaws grinding and her eyes brimming with tears. Then, suddenly, with Uncle Vili's bold head rising, pink in the lamplight, I overheard snatches of his wishful ponderings. I also recall Uncle Lajòs's solemn words, received in complete silence, when he called for God's intervention so that "soon we can all again be able to gather together at the family table in peace, love, and good health."

I was barely able to capture one or two glances from my father. All I noticed about my stepmother was that everyone showed great concern for her, almost more than for my father, and once when she said she had a headache, she was asked if she needed a pill or some compresses, but she wanted neither. At irregular intervals my attention was caught by my grandmother, constantly wandering about and having to be drawn back to the sofa, with her many complaints, her blind eyes—covered by thick glasses clouded over by tears—looking like two bizarre, perspiring insects seen through magnifying glasses. Then, at a predetermined moment, everyone got up from the table. The final good-byes began. My grandmother and grandfather offered their good-byes separately, because they left before my stepmother's family. For me the most memorable moment of the whole evening was perhaps the only noticeable action by my grandfather, when he pressed his small birdlike head for one brief but entirely wild and irrational second against my father's chest. His whole body twisted convulsively.

Then he made a beeline for the door, guiding my grandmother by her elbow. A path opened up for them. Then several guests hugged me too, and I felt the residue of sticky lips on my cheeks. Finally there was a sudden quiet, since everyone had gone.

Then I, too, said good-bye to my father, or rather he said good-bye to me. I'm not sure. I can't recall the circumstances exactly: my father probably stepped outside with some of the guests, because for a short time I stayed alone at the table, which was covered by the remnants of the dinner. I woke up from a doze only when he returned. "Tomorrow at dawn we will not have time for this," he said. Mostly he enumerated my responsibilities and repeated what Uncle Lajos already had said this afternoon about my becoming an adult (except that he did not refer to God and did not use flowery words and was much briefer). He now referred to my mother: he had a suspicion that she would perhaps try to persuade me to leave home and go and live with her. I noticed that this idea really worried him. For the two of them had quarreled forever over my custody, until finally the court had decided in my father's favor; now I fully understood that he didn't want to lose his rights over me simply on account of his unfortunate situation. But he appealed to my reasonableness rather than pleading the law, as he highlighted the difference between my stepmother, who had "created a warm family home" for me, and my mother, who, in contrast, had "deserted" me. I became more attentive, because my mother explained this particular detail very differently; according to her, my father was the one at fault. That was why she was forced to choose another husband, a certain Uncle Dino (in reality, Denes), who, incidentally, had left just the week before, also for a labor camp. But I have never been able to discover the exact turn of events, and even now my father immediately returned to my stepmother, noting that I had her to thank for my no longer being at boarding school and that now my place was here "at home, next to her."

He spoke on and on about her, and now I gathered why my stepmother wasn't present to hear: she would certainly have been embarrassed by his words. They wore me out, though. I can't even remember what I promised my father when he asked me. But then the next moment I found myself suddenly in his arms, and I found his tight hug unexpected; I was somehow unprepared for it after his speech. I don't know whether this was why my tears started flowing or whether sheer exhaustion was the cause or whether perhaps somehow I had been expecting this ever since my stepmother's first warning in the morning, expecting that at this particular moment the tears definitely were going to flow. Whatever the reason, it happened the way it should have. My father also, I sensed, was pleased that it had happened. Then he sent me to bed. I was already very tired. But, so I thought to myself, we were still able to send him, poor dear man, off to labor camp with the memory of a beautiful day.

2

It has been two months now since we said good-bye to my father. Summer is now here, but at school we were given vacations long ago, in the springtime. They explained: we are at war. Airplanes now are flying over us and bombing the city, and they have passed new laws concerning the Jews.

For two weeks now I have been working. I was officially given notice of an "assignment to a permanent work position." The address said, "Georg Koves, young laborer in training," so I knew instantly that the paramilitary youth organization had had a hand in the writing. But I had also heard that this was the way they filled such positions—with people like me, who would otherwise be disqualified from performing labor service because of their age. Eighteen other boys are with me there for the same reason, since they are all around fifteen years old. Our working place is in Csepel, at the Shell Oil Refinery works. In this way I have attained a kind of rare distinction, because usually those of us with yellow stars are prohibited from passing beyond the city limits. But I was given official papers, complete with a stamp by the commander of the military factory giving me "official permission to cross the Csepel border."

The work itself is quite amusing, being relatively easy and therefore allowing me the companionship of the other boys. It consists of unskilled labor in the construction trade. Since the oil refinery has fallen victim to a bombing raid, our job is to try to repair the destruction caused by the airplanes. The foreman who supervises us doesn't treat us badly; at the end of the week he even hands out our wages just as if we were regular workers. But what thrills my stepmother most are the papers, because until now, whenever I went out, she worried constantly about how I'd identify myself if the necessity arose. Now, however, she has no reason to worry, since according to my papers I serve not just my own pleasure but also the military interests of industry. That naturally casts an entirely different light on everything. The whole family has the same opinion. Only my stepmother's sister dared to complain a bit that I was being forced to perform physical labor. She asked, nearly in tears: "Is this why you went to prep school?" My reply was that I thought this activity was beneficial for my health. Uncle Vili agreed completely with me, and Uncle Lajos suggested that, yes, we must not resist what God ordains. After that, she stopped. Then Uncle Lajos took me aside for a serious conversation: among other things he warned me never to forget that while I'm at the workplace I am no longer simply representing myself but "the whole Jewish community" and that therefore I have a responsibility to be on my best behavior for *their* sake because from my particular example they will draw conclusions about all the other Jews. Quite frankly, I doubt that I would have thought of this myself. But then I realized that he probably knew what he was talking about.

My father's letters have arrived regularly from the labor camp. Thank God he is healthy and can endure the work! He is being treated decently, he writes. The family is pleased with the contents of the letters. Uncle Lajos has the opinion that God has watched over my father until now; he urged us to pray daily so that God will continue standing over him, for it is He who holds power over all our lives. In addition, Uncle Vili reassured me that in any case we'll only have to suffer for a "short transitional period," because, as he explained, the landing of the Allied Forces has sealed the fate of the Germans once and for all.

So far I've also been successful in avoiding any disagreements with my stepmother. She, however, has been forced to be idle, the reason being that it was commanded that the business couldn't be run by anyone of impure blood. But it certainly seems that my father played his cards well as far as betting on Mr. Suto is concerned, for every week he has faithfully delivered our portion of the profits from the lumberyard under his control, just as he swore to Father. This last time, too, he was prompt and counted out a tidy sum of money on the table, at least from what I could tell. He kissed my stepmother's hand politely and even had a few friendly words for me. As usual, he asked in great detail about "the boss's" welfare. We were almost ready to say good-bye when he recalled something. He took a package from his briefcase. His face appeared a bit tense. "I hope, dear lady," he said formally, "that you can make use of it around the home." The package was filled with lard, sugar, and other such things. It was my suspicion that he had bought them on the black market, maybe because he too might have read the regulation that all Jews in the future had to content themselves with smaller rations of food. At first my stepmother tried to object, but Mr. Suto kept insisting, and so, naturally, she was unable to raise any further objections to his courteous offer. When we were alone, she asked me if I thought she had acted properly in accepting the package. I replied that I thought she had. She shouldn't offend Mr. Suto by refusing to accept the gift, since, after all, he was only trying to help her. She thought the same thing and suggested that my father would approve of her handling of the situation. Indeed, I didn't think any differently. Anyway, she is usually more knowledgeable about such matters than I am.

I have visited my mother twice a week at the same time in the afternoon. She has caused a lot of trouble. Just as my father had predicted, she refused to agree that my place was with my stepmother. According to her, I "belong" to *her*, my *real* mother. But according to my understanding, the courts declared that I should remain with my father; therefore it is *his* decision that should concern me. In spite of all this, Mother asked me repeatedly this Sunday exactly what I planned to do with my life, because according to her only two things are important: what I plan for my life and whether I love her. I explained that of course I loved her. But according to Mother, to love someone means that one wishes to be near that person, and Mother's impression is that I wish to be near my stepmother. I tried to get her to understand that she had a mistaken impression, because it really wasn't my decision to stay with my stepmother; that was my father's. Her response was that my very life was at stake here, that the decision was mine, and that "one proves one's love by deeds, not words." When I left her, I felt quite troubled: How could I let her think I didn't love her? But how could I take her seriously when she said such things about my being so important and that when it came to my life, I had to be the one making the decisions? The nub of it was that that was their private quarrel, not mine. And anyway, I'd be on emotionally dangerous ground making such decisions. Finally, I can't shortchange my father, especially not now, while the poor man is forced to be in a labor camp. Still, I climbed up onto the streetcar with a heavy heart because, of course, I care for my mother, and I was naturally disturbed that, once again, I was powerless to do much of anything for her.

Maybe my sense of guilt was responsible for my being slow in offering my good-bye to Mother. She was the one who finally insisted, "It's getting late," taking into account that wearers of yellow stars are only free to walk the streets until 8:00 P.M. I explained that since I am now the holder of official papers, I'm free from having to pay such careful attention to each and every regulation.

Still, I made my way to the last row of the last car of the streetcar exactly according to the regulations. At nearly eight o'clock I arrived home, and even though it was summertime and thus still light, some windows were already covered over by black or blue curtains. My stepmother was becoming impatient, but primarily out of habit, because, after all, I now possessed the official papers. We whiled away the evening, as usual, at the Fleischmanns'. The two old men are the same. They continued disagreeing about most things, but they both approved of my going to work, chiefly because of the papers, naturally. In their eagerness to be helpful, they had a minor quarrel. My stepmother and I aren't well acquainted with the Csepel area, so we asked directions from them when I began work. Old Mr. Fleischmann suggested the local streetcar, but Uncle Steiner favored the bus, because, he asserted, it stopped right in front of the refinery, while I would find it necessary to walk some distance from the streetcar stop. As the future later showed, he was right. But we couldn't have known this beforehand, so Uncle Fleischmann was quite annoyed. "You always have to be right," he fussed. Finally the two fat wives were forced to intervene. Anne-Marie and I had some good laughs over them and their quarrels.

With her I ended up in a somewhat peculiar situation. The event occurred during the Friday night air raid at the bomb shelter, or more precisely in one of the deserted half-dark cellar corridors opening from it.

At first I only intended to show her how much more exciting the experience of the outside was from here. But when a minute or two later we heard a bomb exploding nearby, she started trembling all over. I could feel the trembling because in her fright she grabbed me: her arm was hooked around my neck, and her face was buried in my neck. Then I only remember seeking her lips. I felt a little warm, moist, somewhat sticky touch, and then a certain bemused wonderment, because, after all, this was the first time I had ever kissed a girl, and I hadn't even anticipated it.

The next day in the hallway I discovered that she, too, was quite surprised. "It was the bomb," she explained. In essence she was correct. Then we kissed again, and she taught me how, by assigning a certain role to our tongues, we could create a more memorable sensation.

That night we went to the other room to admire Fleischmann's aquarium. Actually, we had gone there regularly to look at the fish. But this time, of course, we didn't go there just to watch the fish. We put our tongues to work. But we came back quickly, because Anne-Marie was nervous that her aunt and uncle might get wind of our little adventure. Later, while we were talking, she let me in on what she thought of me. She said that she had never dreamed I could be anything more than simply a "good friend." At first she'd seen me only as a child. Later, she confessed, she became more attentive to me, and a certain awareness of compatibility with me grew in her, perhaps because of the similar social backgrounds of our parents. Furthermore, she had guessed from a few of my remarks that we saw eye to eye on certain subjects. But that was all, no more. She had no suspicion of anything else. She mused about how strange things were turning out; then she added that perhaps all this was fated.

Her face had a strange, almost strict expression, and I didn't resist hearing her views, even though I tended to agree with yesterday's explanation, namely that the bomb had been responsible. But of course, I don't know much, and from what I could see, the second version was more appealing to her. Soon afterward, we said our good-byes because I had to get up and go to work early the next morning, and as I took her hand in mine, she inflicted a sharp little pain in my palm with her fingernails. I understood that she was hinting at our secret, and her face seemed to imply "Everything is okay."

The next day, however, she acted rather strangely, because in the afternoon, after I returned from work, washed up, changed my shirt and shoes, and combed back my hair, we walked to the sisters' place according to plan (Anne-Marie had taken care of the introductions much earlier). Their mother welcomed us cordially. (Their father is also in a labor camp.) Their flat is "respectable," having a balcony and rugs, two spacious rooms, and a smaller room for the two girls. A piano, several dolls, and other girlish objects are in here. Usually we played cards, but today the older sister was not interested. First, she said, she needed to discuss something that was weighing on her mind, a thing that had consumed her thoughts lately: her yellow star was the cause of all these worries.

To be exact, "the stares and glances thrown my way" raised her awareness of the problem. She had become aware that people's attitudes had changed toward her, for she could now see when she looked in their eyes that they "hated" her. She noticed this look when she was out shopping for her mother. But I think she exaggerated things a little. My own experience, you see, is not exactly the same. For example, at work some of the master bricklayers are noted for disliking Jews, yet with us youngsters they struck up a sort of friendship. At the same time, of course, I'm aware that this alters absolutely nothing as far as their more general attitudes are concerned. Then I also recalled the example of the baker, and I tried to persuade the girl that it was not she, that is, she personally, whom they hated—since after all they'd not even met her—but rather that they hated her (more broadly) as a "Jew." Then she pointed out that this was precisely what weighed on her mind, because quite frankly she had never exactly understood the meaning of that word. And although Anne-Marie told her that everybody knew it just refers to a religion, she wasn't interested in discovering that, but the deeper meaning of the word. After all, "shouldn't one know why one is hated?" she argued. She confessed that initially she had been perplexed and deeply hurt when she sensed rejection "simply because I'm a Jew." That was the very first time she became aware that a gulf separated her from other people and that she belonged somewhere else. Then she began to puzzle over and delve into the subject in books and conversations, and that's when it hit her: this and this thing alone was exactly what they hated in her. For she held the opinion that "we Jews are different from other people," and this difference or otherness is the essence of and rationale about why people detest us.

She also mentioned how odd it was to live with the "consciousness of this otherness" and how she vacillated between pride in it and shame because of it. She eagerly wanted to know how we dealt with our own otherness and whether we were proud or ashamed of it. Her sister and Anne-Marie were uncertain. I myself had seen little reason until now for such feelings. Besides, one can't really determine such a particular otherness oneself; after all, I assumed, that was the function of the yellow star. I mentioned that to her. But she insisted stubbornly, "We carry this otherness within ourselves." I, on the other hand, held that what we wore on the outside was more essential. We argued interminably. I'm not quite sure why, because quite frankly the whole question left me cold. But something about her way of thinking annoyed me. To me all of this is much simpler. Furthermore, I wanted to win the argument, naturally. Once or twice I got the idea that Anne-Marie also wanted to speak up, but we never gave her a chance because we paid little attention to her.

To win the argument, I cited an example. Occasionally, just to pass the time, I had thought about something that now occurred to me. I had read a book, a novel, recently, about a beggar and a prince who resembled each other so closely in face and form that one couldn't tell them apart. Out of mere curiosity they exchanged identities, until finally the beggar became a genuine prince and the prince a genuine beggar. I asked the girl to try placing herself imaginatively in the story. Not, of course, because such a thing is probable, but because many things are theoretically possible. Let's assume, I said, that as a toddler, when she could not talk and would not later remember, somehow (how is immaterial) she had been exchanged, accidentally or intentionally, with the toddler of a family whose papers with regard to racial matters were totally acceptable. Well, in that case, then, it would be the other young woman who would become aware of her otherness and would likewise be wearing the yellow star, while she, because of her documents, would see herself as being exactly like—and others would also view her as exactly like—other people. And she would never consider thinking of or even imagining any sort of otherness.

I noticed that this argument had an effect upon her. Her first reaction was one of guilt, and then, slowly, but so softly that it was almost palpable, her lips parted as if she were trying to tell me something. She didn't, but something else, something more unusual happened: she burst into tears. She burrowed her face in the bend of her elbow, which was resting on the table, and her shoulders contracted in small tremors. I was tremendously astonished, because this hadn't been my slightest intention, and besides, the whole scene left me totally confused. I tried to bend over her and touch her hair and arms and beg her to stop crying. With a cracking voice, she desperately shouted something to the effect that if our distinctiveness was unimportant, then all this was mere chance, and that if there was the possibility of her being someone other than whom she was fated to be, then all this was utterly without reason, and to her that idea was totally "unbearable."

I was embarrassed because I was to blame here. There was no way I could have known how much she valued her ideas. I was just about to tell her, "Don't worry, I couldn't care less either way. I for one don't reject you because of your race," but I could immediately see how ridiculous such a speech would be, so I said nothing. But still I was annoyed that I couldn't speak up, because right then I genuinely felt like it, and her feelings were completely different from my own. This is the way I saw it. But of course, under different circumstances maybe my opinion would have been different too. Who knows? I suddenly realized that I couldn't prove anything. But still, somehow, I felt uncomfortable. Who knows why, but now for the first time I felt something like shame.

Only later on the staircase did I notice that this feeling of mine offended Anne-Marie. This was clear from her strange behavior. I spoke to her, and she didn't respond. I tried to take her arm; she jerked it away and left me there, standing alone on the steps.

The next afternoon I waited in vain for her visit. I couldn't go and see the sisters either, since up until then we had always visited them together, and they would certainly be suspicious if I came alone. Anyway, I began to see more and more clearly what the older sister was driving at during Sunday's conversation.

In the evening Anne-Marie came over to the Fleischmanns'. At first she exchanged some very stiff words with me. Her face relaxed a little only when I replied to her comment that she hoped that I'd had a pleasant afternoon with the sisters; I told her that I hadn't gone there at all. She was curious about why not, and I told her the truth: I had no interest in going alone. My answer apparently pleased her. After a while she was interested in going with me to watch the fish, and from there we again were completely at peace with one another. Later on in the evening she made only one further remark about all this: she told me that this had been our first fight.

3

The next day something strange happened. I got up early, as usual, and started going to work. The day promised to be warm, and the bus was jammed full of passengers. We had already left the suburbs far behind and had crossed the short, plain bridge that leads to Csepel Island. From here the road continues through open fields. To the left is some sort of an open-air shed; to the right, scattered greenhouses. Then it happened. The bus suddenly jerked to a halt, and I overheard a voice outside giving orders that were then relayed to me by the passengers and the conductor: if there were any Jewish passengers on the bus, they had to get off. Well, I thought, they probably wanted to have a crossing check and verify our papers.

In fact, I found myself out on the road face to face with a policeman. Without uttering a word, I handed him my papers. But first he sent the bus on its way with a short flick of his wrist. I was almost ready to believe that maybe he had failed to understand my papers, and I was working myself up to explain to him that, as he could plainly see, I was a working member of the military industry and therefore had little time to waste. But then, suddenly, the road was filled with the voices of boys—my coworkers at Shell. They had been hiding behind an embankment. It turned out that they had been ordered off an earlier bus by the policeman, and they laughed and giggled because I had now become one of them. Even the policeman smiled a bit like someone who, though from a great distance, was still an insider to a joke. I immediately noticed that he had no objections to us. How could he, anyway? Still, I asked the boys what was going on, but they were also in the dark.

The policeman kept stopping all the city buses by stepping onto the road at a safe distance and raising his hand. While he did that, he made sure we were hidden behind the bank. Then, each time, the exact same scene played itself out, and the initial bewilderment of the new boys eventually changed into laughter. The policeman looked satisfied. In this way we passed a quarter of an hour or so. It was a clear summer morning, and on the opposite side of the bank—we felt it as we lay there— the sun began warming the grass. From afar, in the midst of a bluish mist, you could clearly discern the fat drums of the oil refinery. Beyond them were the factory smokestacks, and still further, a great deal more hazily, was the pointed outline of a church steeple. From the buses, alone or in groups, more and more boys arrived. A popular, very lively, freckled boy with black hair cut like a thornbush also arrived: everyone called him Leather-Worker because, unlike the others, who came from various prep schools, he had chosen to learn a profession. Then Smoker came. You could rarely catch him *sans* cigarette. Of course, most of the others smoked too, and to keep from being excluded, I had also tried smoking; but I noticed that he indulged in this habit very differently, with an almost feverish eagerness. His eyes also reflected a strange, feverish expression. He was very sullen; it was hard to reach him emotionally, and he was not especially liked by the boys. But still, I finally ventured once to ask him what good there was in chain-smoking. He answered curtly: "It's cheaper than food." I was a bit taken aback, since that was an answer I hadn't anticipated. But what surprised me even more was a certain sarcastic, almost judgmental expression that showed on his face when he became aware of my confusion. It was definitely unpleasant, and I stopped asking him questions. Then I understood the cautious behavior of the others toward him.

With uninhibited shouts they greeted another boy, who was called Silky Boy by his closer friends. I found the name appropriate because of the silkiness of his straight, shiny dark hair, his large gray eyes, and his amiable personality. I discovered only later that the name carried another meaning and that that's why they had stuck it on him: because he acted very smooth in "intimate settings," that is, around girls. One of the buses also delivered Rozi. His name was really Rosenfeld, but his nickname was Rozi. For some reason he was greatly respected by the boys, and in questions of general concern, we were usually swayed by his opinions. He was also our liaison with the foreman. It was my understanding that he was studying at a business school. He brought to mind the old masterpieces in a museum usually called *Infant with Hound* or some such title, because of his intelligent, though somewhat too-long face, wavy blond hair, and watery blue eyes. Moskovics, a small boy with a plainer (I would almost say rather ugly) face, also arrived. On his flat, wide nose sat metal-ribbed thick glasses, just like my grandmother's. And on and on, others kept arriving.

The general opinion was that the whole business was unusual and probably a mistake (and that's how I too viewed the situation). Encouraged by some of the boys, Rozi did ask the policeman, "Won't there be trouble if we're late for work, and when, in fact, are you planning to let us go on to work?" The policeman was not in the least perturbed by the question and replied that the decision was not his to make. As the future showed, in fact, he knew little more than we did: he briefly referred to certain "further orders" that would supersede the original one, which both he and we now had to wait for. That was basically what he said by way of explanation. All of this, even if it was vague, we all agreed sounded feasible. Besides, we had to obey him. This attitude was all the easier to hold because, being in possession of official papers and the official stamps of the military industry, we saw little reason to take the policeman too seriously—that was quite clear. He, on his part, remarked that he liked to deal with "intelligent boys" on whom he could depend for "disciplined behavior." I was confident that he liked us. He was also very pleasant; he was rather short, neither old nor young, with a sunburnt face and very light, clear eyes. I surmised from some dropped words that he probably hailed from the country.

It was now 7:00 A.M. This was when work started up at the refinery. The buses were not bringing any more boys, and the policeman then asked us, "Is anyone missing?" Rozi reported that all were accounted for. Then the policeman decided that we probably shouldn't wait by the roadside. He looked worried, and somehow I thought that he was as unprepared for us as we were for him. He even asked, "What on earth am I to do with you all?" But of course we couldn't answer that question. We circled him in a completely uninhibited manner, laughing, just as if we were schoolboys with a teacher on a field trip, and he stood at the very center of our group, thinking and stroking his chin. Finally he suggested, "Let's go to the customhouse."

We accompanied him to a worn-down, solitary single-story building right beside the road, the Customhouse, as the weather-beaten inscription told us. The policeman pulled out a ring full of keys, and from them he chose the one that fit the lock. Inside we found a pleasant, cool, spacious, rather empty room, furnished with a few benches and an old, worn-out table. The policeman opened another door leading into a much smaller, officelike room. As I peeked through the cracked door, I noticed that it had a carpet, a desk, and a telephone. We heard him making a phone call. Although we couldn't quite make out the words, I believe he was trying to speed up the orders, because when he returned and carefully pulled the door shut behind him, he said: "Nothing, all for nothing. We have to wait." He urged us to make ourselves at home. He wanted to know if we knew any group games. One of the boys—I think it was Leather-Worker—suggested the game of red meat. The policeman, however, didn't approve of this game and said he expected more from us since we were "such intelligent children." For a while he joked around with us, and I had the clear impression that he was trying his level best to amuse us somehow, maybe in order to make sure that we wouldn't think of being unruly, as he had mentioned a while back; but he seemed quite inexperienced in such matters. So he left us to our own devices soon after he said that he had to return to his work. After he left, we heard the door being locked behind him.

My memory of any later events is all hazy. It seemed we waited and waited for the orders. But all in all, we were in no great hurry. After all, we weren't wasting *our* time. And we all agreed on one thing: we found more pleasure staying here in the cool than sweating at work. The oil refinery did not have any shade. Rozi had been successful in getting the foreman's permission for us to remove our shirts. Admittedly that failed to comply with the letter of the law, because in this way our yellow stars couldn't be seen, but the foreman had still given us permission—out of his humanity. Only Moskovics's paperlike white skin was the worse for it, because his shoulders immediately turned lobster red, and we laughed uproariously about the long strips of skin that he peeled off his back.

We settled ourselves in as comfortably as possible on the benches or simply on the floor of the customhouse, but it'd be impossible for me to recall what we did with all that time. Anyway, several jokes were told, and cigarettes and later lunch boxes came out. We talked about the foreman: we talked about how he had to be quite surprised at not seeing us at work that morning. Horseshoe nails were found, and so we could play bull. I learned a game there among the boys: someone throws a nail high up in the air, and the one who grabs the most nails from the pile in front of him before he catches his nail again wins. Silky Boy, with his long fingers and narrow hands, always won this game. Rozi also taught us a song, which we sang a lot. Its appeal was that it could be translated into three different languages, even though the words stayed the same: with an *es* attached, every word sounded German; with an *io,* Italian; and with *taki,* Japanese. Of course all these pastimes were silly, but they amused me.

Then I focused my attention on the grown-ups. The policeman was now rounding them up from the buses, just as he had done with us. I saw that when he was not with us, he was out on the road, engaged in the same activity as he had been in the morning. Gradually seven or eight people were collected, all of them men. But I noticed they gave the policeman more trouble than we had; they fussed, shook their heads, offered long explanations, kept showing their papers, kept pestering him with questions. They also examined us: who and what were we? But mostly they kept to themselves. We gave them a couple of benches. There they either squatted or stood around. They talked incessantly, but I paid little attention to them. Chiefly they tried to analyze the reason for the policeman's actions and the consequences these events would have on them individually. As far as I could make out, however, their opinions were just as varied as the people. Chiefly, from what I could tell, their opinions depended on the kinds of papers they carried, because, as I understood the situation, their papers were given to them because their destination was also Csepel—some for private reasons, and others, like ours, for official reasons.

I noticed a few faces full of character. For instance, I saw that one of the men held himself aloof from the conversation and kept reading a book that he happened to be carrying. He was a lanky, skinny man with a yellow trench coat, and a severe line that substituted for his mouth was placed between two deep, glum-looking indentations. He chose a spot on the edge of one of the benches next to the window. There he stayed with his legs crossed and his back half turned to the others. Maybe that was why he recalled to my mind a seasoned train traveler who considers every word, question, or the usual petty socializing among occasional travelers entirely useless and suffers the journey with a bored composure. At least he struck me that way.

There was also a well-dressed, somewhat older gentleman with thinning hair and graying temples who already upon his arrival—at midmorning, approximately—captured my eye, for he was objecting vehemently as the policeman ushered him in. He even begged to use a telephone. The policeman, however, replied that, regrettably, the phone was "strictly for official use." At that the man became quiet but no less annoyed. Later I found out from his curt responses to the questions of others that he too belonged to one of the Csepel factories. He referred to himself as an "expert adviser" but refrained from going into any details. He appeared openly self-confident, and I thought his attitudes were generally similar to ours except that he seemed to take the delay as a personal insult. I noticed that he constantly belittled the policeman, speaking patronizingly about him. He thought that the policeman had some vague instructions, "which he was pursuing with over-eagerness." He believed, though, that eventually his own situation would be dealt with by "professionals," and with luck this would be very soon—the sooner the better. Then I heard little more from him and put him out of my mind. Only in the afternoon did he again bring himself to my attention, but by then I too was tired and only noticed how impatient he seemed to be. He kept sitting down and then standing up, crossing his arms on his chest, then behind his back, and then glancing down at his watch.

There was also an odd little man with a very pronounced nose and a mammoth knapsack who was wearing golf pants and gigantic boots. Even the yellow star on him seemed larger than the ones on all the others. He constantly worried. He complained to everyone about his bad luck. I can recall his story reasonably well, because it was simple and he stated it over and over. He was going to pay a visit to his "very sick" mother in the Csepel community, so he informed us. He had managed to receive a special dispensation from the authorities that he carried and that he passed around to us. The dispensation was only valid for today and only until 2:00 P.M. But something had come up, he said, something that he had to attend to, that couldn't be postponed, and he added, "for business reasons." But the office he had to visit was crowded, and so he was forced to wait for what seemed like forever. He had seen the whole trip endangered, he said. Still, he had rushed and hopped on a train so that he could arrive at the bus station according to his original plan. Along the way, though, he weighed the pros and cons—the time required for the trip, the duration of his permit—and he decided that getting started on the journey was a risky business. But while waiting at the bus station, he noticed a bus destined for the south, and then he thought to himself what unbelievable difficulty this insignificant little piece of paper had cost him, and, he added, "poor Mama is expecting me." He informed us that the old woman was most assuredly the source of a bundle of trouble for both him and his wife. They had been appealing to her constantly to come and live with them in the city. But his mother kept refusing, until finally every chance was lost. He shook his head because he steadfastly believed that the old woman just hoped to hold on to her own house "at any price," even though, he said, it lacked indoor facilities. But, he continued, he had to be understanding, for she *was* his mother. And poor dear, he added, she was sick, and also old. He said he felt he would never manage to forgive himself if he neglected this sole chance of looking in on her. So finally he did climb up onto the bus.

Then he became numb momentarily. He lifted his hand and then allowed it to fall slowly in a hopeless gesture, while a multitude of minuscule wrinkles appeared on his forehead. He reminded me of a melancholy rodent in a trap. He asked the others if they had the opinion that he might get into trouble. Or would the authorities take into consideration that passing over the permitted time frame was not his fault? And what could his mother, who had been informed of his impending visit, possibly be imagining, and what would his wife and his two infants think if he failed to return home by two o'clock? Mostly, it seemed to me, judging from the direction of his glances, he was asking for the thoughts or comments of the proper-looking "expert adviser." This gentleman, however, paid little attention to him, I noticed. He held a cigarette in his fingers; he had just removed it and was tapping its end against the ornate top of his glittering silver case. I saw a reflective expression on the "expert's" face; he seemed lost in distant thoughts and probably had heard nothing of the whole tale. The other man then lapsed back into lamenting his bad fortune: if perhaps he had arrived at the bus station five minutes later, then he wouldn't have caught the bus; if he had not caught the bus, then he wouldn't have stood waiting for the next one; and so, "provided all these ifs had happened within a five-minute time span," he would now be sitting "not here but at home." With only his lips moving, this is what he kept repeating soundlessly, again and again.

I also recall a man with a seal's face. He was fat. He had a thick black mustache and gold-rimmed spectacles. He was constantly trying to talk with the policeman. It didn't escape my attention that he always tried this while alone, whenever possible, in a corner or at the door. "Sir Officer," I heard his whispering, throaty voice say, "may I please talk to you?" Or "Sir Officer, with your permission, if it's possible, just a word." Finally the policeman asked him what was on his mind. Then he seemed to hesitate. At first his spectacles scanned the room suspiciously. And even though the man stood in a corner of the room fairly near me, I couldn't make anything out of his muffled mumblings. He seemed to be protesting about something. Then a certain confidential, sugary smile appeared on his face, and at the same time he gradually turned around and approached the policeman. At the same time I noticed a strange motion of his. I didn't completely comprehend it at first; it seemed as if he was trying to reach for something in his inside pocket. I judged by the obvious significance that he attached to his gesture that he was eager to give the policeman some important papers or some extraordinary or unusual document. But I waited in vain to see if he had anything, because he never completed the motion. He didn't completely freeze either, however. Instead, his arm became suspended, forgotten, sort of stuck in midair. And so, eventually, his hands were running up and down and scratching toward the policeman's breast. He looked like a big hairy spider or rather like a small sea monster looking for a chink through which to penetrate the policeman's coat. During this time he talked on and on, as that particular smile remained frozen on his face. This lasted just a few seconds. Then I was struck by how the policeman quickly, and in a strikingly determined manner, ended the conversation. In fact, I thought he was quite offended, and indeed, even though quite honestly I didn't understand much of what had occurred, still in some indescribable way I found the man's behavior objectionable.

The other faces and other events are all hazy. Besides, as time passed, my observations gradually lessened in sharpness. I could tell, though, that the policeman remained attentive to us boys. With the grown-ups, however, he became a shade less cordial. By the afternoon he too seemed exhausted. He stayed in the shade with us or sometimes stayed in his room and ignored the buses passing by. I heard him try phoning several times. Once or twice he reported the outcome: "Still nothing." But now he reported the results with frustration written all over his face.

I recall one other event. It happened earlier, around noon. The policeman was visited by a buddy, another policeman on a bike. He left the bike in the room leaning against the wall. Then they locked themselves in our policeman's office. They stayed there for quite a while. They were talking as they emerged, saying good-bye again and again. They didn't speak, but nodded and glanced at each other, as I recall, like merchants in my father's office in the past when they had complained about hard times and slow business. Of course, I realized that this wasn't a likely topic among policemen, but still, their faces conjured up this memory in my mind: the same expression of worried concern and the same inevitable acceptance of the unalterable order of things. But I was beginning to feel worn out. All I remember of the remaining time was that I was hot, I was bored, and I was getting sleepy.

All in all, the day finally ended with some orders arriving at four o'clock sharp, just as the policeman had promised. They said we were to head straight for the authorities to present our papers to them, as the policeman informed us. He must have been given his orders by phone, because prior to his informing us, we overheard his hurried voice coming from his room, referring to some change of plans. The phone rang urgently several times, and he, too, tried several connections and made brief, determined-sounding comments. The policeman also assured us that, even though he wasn't given the details exactly, he was firmly convinced that cases as clear and legally unequivocal as, for example, ours would simply be a formality.

We walked out in rows of three, heading back toward the city, starting out, as I later discovered during the march, at the same time as others from all of the other border checkpoints. After we crossed the bridge, we were joined at the crossings and curves by other groups of yellow-starred people and one or two, and once even three, policemen. In one of these groups I recognized the policeman with the bike. I also noticed that on each occasion the policemen greeted each other with the same almost workmanlike curtness, like those anticipating a meeting, and then I understood our policeman's arrangements on the phone earlier: it seems he was coordinating the times of meeting with all the others. Finally I found myself marching in the midst of a sizable row. On both sides at irregular intervals, policemen bordered our group.

So we walked, always in the street, for a rather long time. It was a beautiful clear summer afternoon. The streets were resplendent with color, as usual at this time of day. But I saw all this as somewhat blurred. I also lost my sense of direction, because we were mostly crossing streets and roads with which I wasn't particularly familiar. And then the increasing number of streets, the traffic, but mostly the difficulties that necessarily result from such a group marching occupied most of my attention and quickly exhausted me. What I remember best of the long journey is the reaction of the pedestrians watching our march: they had a kind of hurried, hesitant, almost furtive curiosity. At first this amused me, but later I lost interest in it. And I also remember a later, somewhat confused moment. We were walking along a very busy suburban street surrounded by the honking, unbearably loud flow of traffic; at one point, I don't know how, a streetcar wedged itself into our group but far ahead of my row. We were forced to halt for the minute it took it to cross in front of us, and then my attention was caught by the sudden darting flash of a yellow piece of clothing up front, in the vapors of dust and the noise from the vehicles.

I was startled. Somehow this sudden movement didn't jibe with the man's behavior back at the customhouse, I thought. But at the same time I also had another feeling, some sort of a marveling amusement at the sheer simplicity of his act, and indeed, I noticed that one or two other adventurous men immediately took off with him. I gazed around too, but only for the fun of it, let's say, for after all, I couldn't see any other reason for trying to escape. I think I had enough time for it, but still my sense of honor proved to be the stronger of the two urges. And then the policemen quickly took charge, and the rows closed around me.

We walked for a while, and then everything happened quickly and unexpectedly and was a little puzzling. We turned in somewhere, and I figured that we must have reached our destination, because we followed the road between the wide-open wings of a large entrance gate. Beyond the gate I noticed that people other than the policeman came alongside us. They were dressed like soldiers but with more colorful feathers on their simple caps. They were military policemen. They led us deeper into a labyrinth of gray buildings, further and further inside to a gigantic courtyard covered by gravel. It looked like the yard of a military base to me. Then I also noticed a tall, commanding presence making a beeline for us from the opposite building. He wore high boots and a form-fitting uniform with gold stars; a leather belt was strapped across his chest. I saw a thin rod in one of his hands, the type they use for riding, and he used it to tap his shiny boots. A minute later, as we waited motionlessly in row formation, I also noticed that he was a handsome man in his own way. His hardened, manly features reminded me of the handsome heroes in movies. He had a stylishly trimmed, narrow brown mustache, which suited his sunburnt face very well.

As he approached us more closely, we all froze at the guards' commands. From all that followed, I can recall only two impressions. The first was the rasping voice of the man with the riding stick, who reminded me a bit of a market or town crier. His voice surprised me, since it was in such sharp contrast to his professional appearance, and thus I grasped very little from all his words. I understood, though, that he intended to conduct our examination (this was his term) the next day. Then he turned back again to the guards, and in a booming voice that filled the whole square he ordered that they were to carry the "whole band of Jews" to the horse stables to be locked up for the night, where, in his opinion, they belonged anyway. The second impression I remember concerned the impenetrable chaos of loud commands, the shouting directives of the suddenly lively military policemen as they led us away. I didn't know where to turn. I only remember that in the midst of all this I had an urge to laugh, partly because of my astonishment and confusion, partly from the feeling that I had unexpectedly dropped into the middle of an absurd theater play where I didn't know my exact role, and partly because of a passing image that caught my imagination: the face of my stepmother when she realized that she wouldn't have me at home for dinner that night.

4

On the train the thing we missed the most was water. About food: according to all our calculations we had provisions for a long time, but we had nothing to wash it down with, and that was unpleasant. Those who were already on the train let us know immediately that the first thirst disappears quickly. Eventually you almost forget about it; then it reappears. Only the second thirst doesn't let you forget, they explained. For a period of six to seven days, the experts said, a man in warm weather can live without water, provided he is healthy and doesn't perspire too much and refrains from eating meat or spices. For the moment, they encouraged us, there was time. Everything depended on the length of the journey.

That was something I really wanted to know myself: we weren't given that information back in the brick factory in Budakalász. There they only announced that whoever wanted to could apply for work in Germany, and like the rest of the boys and many others there, I immediately appreciated the idea. Besides, an organization called the Jewish Council, whose members were recognizable by the armbands they wore, told us that one way or another, by free will or by force, sooner or later everyone was going to be relocated from the brick factory to Germany. The first volunteers would have better positions with further advantages, since they'd be able to travel with only sixty people per boxcar, while later there would be at least eighty because of the insufficient number of trains. They explained this to everyone. There was therefore really not much room for consideration. That was clear enough.

I couldn't contradict the validity of the other arguments either: those concerning the scarcity of space at the brick factory, the resulting sanitary and health problems, as well as the growing food problems. All of this was true. To that I could testify. Even when we arrived from the military headquarters (many of the grown-ups thought that it was the Andrassy barracks), we found every nook and cranny of the brick factory already jammed full of people. I saw equal numbers of men and women, children of all ages, and countless elderly people of both sexes. Wherever I stepped, I bumped against covers, knapsacks, all kinds of suitcases, and bundles. All of this and the constant complaints, annoyances and inconveniences inevitably associated with such close living, quickly exhausted me, of course. Add to this the idleness, the feeling of wasting one's time and of being bored; that's why I don't remember the five days I spent there individually, and even from their totality I can recall only very little. I do recall being relieved that the other boys were there around me: Rozi and Silky Boy, Leather-Worker, Smoker, Moskovics, and all the others. It seemed that no one was missing: they too were honorable. I didn't have much personal contact with the military policemen. Instead, I saw them standing guard outside the fence, and here and there a few civil policemen were in their midst.

It was said in the brick factory that the civil policemen were much more reasonable than the military policemen and tended to be more humane, especially in response to agreed arrangements, whether of the monetary kind or for other valuables. Sometimes, I heard, people paid them to send messages and letters. Also, some people assured us, there were some rare and risky, but nevertheless real opportunities through them for escape, though it would have been next to impossible to get any definite information concerning this. Then I remembered and also understood somewhat better, I think, what the man with the seal face tried so hard to discuss with the policeman at the customhouse. And this was also how I realized that our police-man was honorable. This explained the fact that, roaming about in the yard or waiting in line at the communal kitchen among the churning multitude of strange faces, I once or twice recognized the seal-faced man.

From among the people at the customhouse, I saw the man with the bad luck too. Frequently he sat among us young people to "cheer myself up a bit," as he said. He must have found a place close to us in one of the brick factory's identical, roofed but otherwise open-sided buildings that, I was told, were originally used for drying the bricks. He looked a bit exhausted—his face was swollen and full of colorful bruises—and he told us they were the consequences of the guards' exam-ination: they had found, in fact, that he had medicine and food in his knapsack. He had tried in vain to explain that all the stuff was old and that he had intended it for his sick mother. They accused him of dealing on the black market. It was useless to explain that he had his permit and that, for his part, he had always respected the law and had never bent a single letter of it.

He usually approached us asking, "Have you heard any-thing? What will happen to us?" He also talked about his family and his bad luck. "How hard I tried to get the permit," he recalled, shaking his head sadly. In no way would he have believed that his affairs would end this way. Everything hinged on those fatal *five* minutes. If he hadn't had bad luck . . . if the bus hadn't . . . I kept hearing these reflections from him. With his punishment, on the other hand, he seemed quite satisfied. "I kept to the rear, and maybe that was my luck," he let us know. "By then they were hurrying up." He summed up the situation by saying that he could have come out a lot worse. He added that he saw "some uglier" cases at the military barracks, and this was, indeed, true. I remember it myself.

On the morning of the examination at the barracks, the military policemen reminded us that "no one should think that he can hide his guilt, his money, his gold or other valuables" from them. When it was my turn, I also had to place my money, watch, pocketknife, and everything else in front of them on the table. A big military policeman also searched me with quick and professional-looking movements from my armpits to the legs of my short pants. Behind the desk I saw the lieutenant, for it became clear from the words exchanged between the military policemen that the name of the man with the riding stick was Lieutenant Szakal. To his left, I noticed, there towered a walrus-mustached, butcher-shaped policemen in shirtsleeves with a cylindrical and fundamentally ridiculous instrument reminiscent of a cook's rolling pin in his hand. The lieutenant asked in a quite friendly way if I had any papers, and I didn't see any sign, any spark of recognition caused by my documents. I was astonished, but seeing the walrus-mustached military policeman's motion of dismissal and his unmistakable gesture of further action if I didn't leave, I thought it more intelligent to object to nothing, of course.

Then the military policemen marched us all from the barracks and stuffed us into some special trains. Then, somewhere along the Danube, they packed us on a ship, and after we landed, they marched us on the final stretch of the journey. This is how I ended up at the brick factory, or more precisely, as I found out when I was there, the Budakalász Brick Factory.

I heard many more things about the journey on the afternoon of the registration. The men with the armbands were everywhere and were glad to answer questions. First and foremost they were seeking out young and enterprising people who were alone. But they assured the people who asked, as I learned, that there was space for women, children, and elderly and that they could carry their packages with them. Yet they considered the most important question to be whether we were interested in taking care of our own affairs and experiencing every possible humaneness, or whether we'd prefer that the military policemen make such decisions for us. For, as they explained, the freight train had to be full, and if *they* didn't fill up their lists, the military policemen would select the cargo. Indeed, most of us—me included—thought we would obviously be better off if we held fast to the first scenario.

Different views also reached me about the Germans. Several

people (mostly the more worldly, older ones) thought that, regardless of how the Germans felt about Jews, basically, as everyone knows, they were clean, honest, orderly, precise, and industrious people who respected others who exhibited these same traits. In general this was also my opinion of them, and I figured that certainly I'd be able to take advantage of having acquired a smattering of their language at school. For the most part, however, I was expecting more order, work, an occupation, and some fun. All in all I hoped for a life-style that was more sensible and more appealing than this one, just as they had promised us and as we boys had figured out among ourselves. Besides all this, I also figured that I'd get to travel and see a bit of the world. To tell the truth, when I reflected on some of the events of the last days, especially the deal with my papers, or about justice in general, my patriotism didn't particularly hold me back.

There were those who were more suspicious, who had different information, and who claimed to know other German qualities. There were others who wanted specific details. There were still others who argued in favor of rational, dignified, exemplary behavior in front of the authorities, instead of quarrels. All these arguments and counterarguments and all sorts of other news and information were discussed and argued in the yard in smaller or larger but constantly dispersing and then re-forming groups. I also heard God invoked; among all the other arguments was "His inscrutable will," as someone put it. Just like Uncle Lajos, this man also spoke about the Jewish fate, and like Uncle Lajos, he believed that we had "turned our faces from the Lord" and that this was the explanation for our trials and tribulations. He got my attention because he was a man of forceful presence and matching build, with a somewhat unusual face characterized by a thin but large curved nose, very shiny, moist-looking eyes, and a handsome graying mustache that touched his short round beard. I noticed that many people surrounded him and were eager to listen to him. I only later heard that he was a priest, because I heard others call him Rabbi.

I noted some of his words and phrases: for example, he conceded that "the eye that sees and the heart that feels" forced him to admit that "we are here on earth perhaps partaking in a measure of the judgment," and his otherwise clean, resonant voice broke and fell silent for a minute, during which time his eyes became even moister than usual. I don't understand why, but I had the strange feeling that he had begun to say something quite different initially and that these words somehow surprised even him. But still, "I didn't want to deceive myself," he confessed. He knew well enough, he said. He only needed to look around and see "this miserable place and these tortured faces" to realize how difficult his job was. I was quite surprised by his sympathy, because, after all, he too was in this very same place with us. But it was not his purpose, he said, since all reason was lacking, "to win souls for the Almighty" because we had already received our souls from Him. He implored all of us: "Do not quarrel with the Lord!" We should avoid this not only because it is sinful but also because that road would lead us "to deny the noble purpose in life" and, conversely, from his point of view, we couldn't live with such a denial in our hearts. "Such hearts," he said, "may be light, but light only because they are empty like the desolate emptiness of the desert. The difficult and only road is the road of solace, namely the recognition of the endless wisdom of the eternal Lord even in tribulations, because," as he put it, "the moment of His victory shall come, and those who denied His might and power shall be united in contrition and shall call to Him from the dust." And so he told us to "believe in the coming of His final mercy, and this belief is to be the unceasing source of our support and strength in this hour of tribulation," and he also suggested the only means by which we could have any existence. He called this means "the denial of denial," because we are "lost," without hope, and, on the other hand, we can receive hope only from the faith and from the unshakable conviction that the Lord will show mercy to us and that we can win His grace. His logic, I admit, seemed quite clear, but I noticed that he never let us know exactly what we were supposed to do, and he wasn't able to give any good advice to those who asked for his opinion on whether they should volunteer for the journey now or stay on here.

I saw the man with the bad luck too, and I noticed that a worried glance from his small, somewhat bloodshot eyes darted tirelessly from one group to another. Occasionally I could hear his voice as he stopped some people and with a tense, probing expression and the cracking of fingers asked if perhaps they too were planning on traveling and why (if he was permitted to ask) was it, in their opinion, better that way.

Right then another acquaintance from the customhouse appeared—as I recall—in order to register. It was the "expert adviser." I had spotted him several times during the brick factory days. Even though his clothes were wrinkled, his tie had disappeared, and his face was covered with a sprouting gray beard, everything about his presence still commanded unquestionable respect. I noticed his presence immediately, because he was surrounded by a ring of excited people who were beleaguering him with a multitude of questions. As I was soon informed, he had had the opportunity of speaking directly with a German officer. The conversation had taken place at the command post near the military policemen's offices and other Secret Service posts, where I did indeed catch sight of an occasional German uniform hurrying by. At first, so I gathered, he had made every effort to speak with the military policemen. He had tried, he said, to contact his firm. But the military policemen had consistently denied him this right, even though he worked for a military establishment and "the supervision of the production" was inconceivable without him. This was recognized by the authorities, even though he had been "robbed" of the relevant documents, as he had been of everything else, at the barracks.

All this I followed with difficulty, because he told his story in bits and pieces, often answering some repetitive questions. He looked outraged. But he remarked, "I don't want to go into details." This is why he had turned to the German officer. The officer was just about to leave. By chance, the adviser informed us, he happened to be nearby. "I placed myself in front of him," he said. There were several witnesses to the event who testified to his foolhardiness. "But," he replied, shrugging his shoulders, "nothing ventured, nothing gained." He wanted "finally to speak with someone in authority, come what may." "I am an engineer," he had said, "and a German." He had laid out everything to the officer. He had informed him that his work was made "impossible both physically and morally" and that all this was being done "entirely illegally, entirely outside the confines of the present regulations. Who profits from this?" he had asked the German officer. He had added, as he told us, "I am not seeking preferential treatment. But I am somebody, and I know something. I'd like to work according to my abilities. That's all I ask."

Then the officer advised him to enlist among the volunteers. The officer was not making any liberal promises, but he assured him that under the present circumstances, which required superhuman effort, Germany needed everyone and especially experts like him. Therefore, he felt, because of the officer's "objectivity," that this was the "correct and realistic" choice. Those were his exact words. He also made special mention of the officer's manners. In stark contrast to the "boorishness" of the military policemen, the officer, as he described him, was "realistic, reasonable, and in every way unobjectionable." Responding to another question, he did admit that "of course there is no other guarantee" than his impression of this lone officer, but he said that for the time being he would have to make do with this, and he doubted that he was mistaken. "Provided," he added, "that my knowledge of people does not entirely deceive me." But he spoke in such a way that I, for one, considered that possibility rather unlikely.

When he left, I suddenly saw the man with the bad luck spring up like a mechanical puppet from the group starting after the adviser, or rather rushing to stand directly in front of him. I thought to myself, judging from the obvious excitement and determination on his face, "Well, now he will speak up to him, the way he didn't back in the customhouse." But instead he bumped into a corpulent colossus of a man with an armband hurrying along with his list and a pencil. The man stopped him and, acting startled, looked him over from head to toe, bent forward, and asked him something—and then I don't know what happened because Rozi called out to us that our turn had come.

All I can remember is that when we boys started walking toward our sleeping places, we saw a particularly peaceful, warm sunset burning rosily above the hills on that final day there. On the other side, the green tops of the local train whizzed by above the fence. I was tired and, since I had registered myself, naturally a little curious. The boys, all in all, seemed satisfied. The man with the bad luck also joined us and said somewhat solemnly (but also with an inquisitive expression on his face) that he, too, was now on the list. We gave him our approval, and I thought this pleased him. But then, I didn't listen much to him. Here in the more distant area of the brick factory everything was quieter. I did see some smaller groups here too—some discussing the day's events and some preparing for the night or having supper or guarding their bags or simply sitting around, quietly, in the night.

We passed by a married couple. I had often seen them and knew them by sight. The wife was small, with fine lines and a fragile frame; the husband was lanky, with eyeglasses and gaps in his teeth, constantly on the run, always rushing, always perspiring on his forehead. Now he was totally occupied: squatting on the ground and eagerly assisted by his wife, he was hurriedly collecting and tying together all their packages; he was constantly absorbed in this activity and noticed nothing else. The man with the bad luck stopped behind him, and it seemed that he knew him, because after a minute he observed, "Well, are you going to move too?" The young man glanced up at him for only a second over his glasses, perspiring with a tightly drawn face in the evening light and replying with a simple sentence: "We'll have to go, won't we?" And I found that observation as true as it was simple.

The next day they sent us on our way early in the glorious

summer weather. The train started out in front of the gate on the tracks of the local train. It was some kind of freight train with brick-red boxcars closed on the top and on the sides. Inside our car there were sixty of us, with packages and provisions supplied by the men with the armbands, mountains of bread and large cans of meat; as seen from brick factory eyes, these were rare, precious commodities, I have to admit. I had noticed since the day before how attentively, deferentially—I would almost say respectfully—they surrounded us, the departing group, and the gracious supplies could have been a sign of that or even some sort of a reward, I felt. The military policemen were there too, armed and buttoned to the chin, rude and unfriendly, as if they were guarding some desired commodity but one that they no longer could touch. I figured that this must be because of some higher authority, perhaps the Germans. Then they closed the door on us and hammered away on the outside. Then there was a whistle, then some sighs, some railroad working, a jolt, and we started to roll. We boys settled down well in the first third of the car, which we occupied as soon as we entered; it was bordered by two high, windowlike openings carefully covered by wire. Soon, in all the cars, questions arose about water and then about the length of the journey.

Other than that, there is little to say about the trip. As in the customhouse and the brick factory, we had to while away the time somehow. What made this task a little more difficult here was, of course, the circumstances. On the other hand, the knowledge of our destination and the thought that everything (regardless of how slow, how tiring, and how bumpy), all the shoving and jostling and waiting, was still just a portion of the journey that would bring us ever closer to our destination helped us to rise above all the difficulties and troubles. We boys kept our patience too. Rozi encouraged us: a journey only lasts until we arrive. They teased Silky Boy a lot too because of—so the boys claimed—a girl who was here with her parents, whom he had met at the brick factory and on whose account, especially at the journey's beginning, he often disappeared into the center of the car. The boys discussed this a lot. Smoker was here too, and even here he took some suspicious-looking remnants and paper from his pocket and also a matchstick, bending his face toward the light with the greediness of a predatory bird at night. Moskovics (his forehead bathed by rivers of sweat mixed with soot that dripped down over his glasses, his short stumpy nose, and his thick lips—sweating like all of us, me included, of course) and the others offered some cheerful words and observations even on the third day. Leather-Worker cracked a few jokes, even if his tongue was now rather slow.

I'm completely ignorant how (but some adults did discover it) we learned that our journey's end was a place named Waldsee. When I was thirsty or hot, the promise contained in that name immediately invigorated me. Those who complained of the overcrowding were reminded that the next load would have eighty persons per car. And really, when I gave it a good thinking over, I had to admit that I had been more crowded before: in the military policemen's stables, for example, where we were only able to solve the space problem by agreeing to squat on the ground in the Turkish fashion. On the train I could sit more comfortably. And if I so desired, I could even get up and walk—for example, in the direction of the pot. This was situated in the distant corner of the car. First we agreed if possible that we'd make use of it for urinating only, but with time the call of nature proved stronger than our earlier resolve, and acting according to nature was for me, the men, and the women only natural.

The military policemen didn't create much unpleasantness either. At first I was a little scared when, directly above my head in the left window, one's face suddenly appeared; he looked down on us with his flashlight during the evening, or rather during the night of the first day on one of our extended stops. But as we soon discovered, he had the best intentions. "Men," he said to us, "you've reached the Hungarian border." He wanted to use this occasion to make an appeal to us. It was his wish, he said, in case we still had some money or valuables, for us to hand them over to him. Specifically, it was his opinion that we had no need of these where we were going. And he assured us that everything we might still hold on to would be taken from us by the Germans anyway. In that case, he emphasized from high up in the window opening, why shouldn't these things find their final resting place in Hungarian, rather than German, hands?

After a momentary pause, which I assumed was in some way meant to be quite solemn, he picked up again in a suddenly warmer, more familiar, and to a certain degree all-forgiving, all-forgetting tone of voice: "After all, you are still Hungarians." In reply, a voice, a deep male voice, rose from the boxcar's bowels, and after some whisperings and calculations, it recognized the validity of the military policeman's argument, provided that as an exchange we should be provided with some water. The military policeman seemed willing enough, although this was "contrary to a clear prohibition." But finally they couldn't settle the disagreement, because the voice insisted on having the water first and the military policeman the valuables, and neither yielded, each insisting on his own sequence of events. Finally the furious military policeman concluded: "Stinking Jews, you make a business out of even the holiest of things!" And in a voice choking with outrage and disgust, he added this wish: "Die of thirst, then!"

Later, incidentally, that did indeed happen. At least that is what some of those in our car reported. And in truth I couldn't avoid hearing a distinct voice from the car directly behind us from the second afternoon on. It wasn't particularly pleasant. An old woman, so those in the know said, was sick and presumably had gone mad with thirst. The explanation sounded plausible. Only then did I grasp the simple truth spoken by some who observed at the journey's outset how lucky we were that there were no babies or old people or sick people traveling in our car. On the morning of the third day the old woman finally fell silent. It was said that she died because she had been given no water. But we knew that she was sick and old; under these circumstances everyone, myself included, thought the event was completely understandable.

I have to say that waiting is not conducive to joy. At least that was my experience when we finally reached our destination. Possibly I was tired, and also perhaps the very eagerness with which I had looked forward to the journey's end helped me to forget this finally, but I was baffled by it all and missed the whole event somehow. I only remember that I was startled from my sleep by the senseless screams of some nearby sirens. A weak light filtering through from the outside already signaled the dawning of the fourth day. The small of my back hurt a bit where it had pressed against the floor of the boxcar. The train had stopped often for other reasons, and always for air raids. The windows, too, were always crowded with people. Everybody claimed to be seeing something. This was par for the course during those days.

After a while I also found a place at the window. I saw nothing. Dawn outside was cool and fragrant. A gray mist hovered over the wide fields, and then unexpectedly, but just like the sound of a trumpet, a thin sharp red ray appeared from behind somewhere, and I understood that I was seeing the sunrise. It was beautiful and quite interesting: at home I usually slept during this hour. I also spotted a building, directly to my left, an abandoned station or perhaps the forerunner of a larger station. It was tiny, gray, and entirely deserted, with small, closed windows and with that ridiculously steep roof that I had been seeing ever since yesterday. Before my very eyes it solidified into a concrete outline in the misty dawn, changing from gray to lilac, and then all at once its windows glistened red as the first rays struck them. Others observed this too, and I recounted it all to the curious. They asked if I could see a name above it. I did: namely, I saw the words in the early light on the narrower side of the building facing in our direction under the roof. Auschwitz-Birkenau was what I read, written in the fancy ornate letters of the Germans, with the two words connected by a double-curved hyphen. I for one canvassed my geographic knowledge in vain; others proved no wiser than I about the place. Then I sat down, because people behind me were asking for my place and because it was still early, and since I was tired, I soon fell asleep once more.

Then I was awakened by movements and excitement. Outside the sun shone in its full glory. The train was moving again. I asked the boys about our location, and they replied, "Still there. We just began moving." So I must have been jolted awake. But without a doubt, they added, directly in front of us one could see factories and some kind of settlement. A minute later, those stationed in front of the window reported, and I also noticed by the alteration in light, that we must have slid through some sort of an arched gateway. After another minute the train stopped, and then the viewers excitedly let us know that they could make out a station, soldiers, and people. Several persons immediately began gathering up their belongings and buttoning up; the women especially began cleaning up, prettying up, and combing themselves. Outside, however, I heard approaching knocks, the slamming of doors, and the jumbled noise of departing passengers, and I was now forced to realize that without a doubt we had indeed arrived at our destination. I was glad, naturally, but I felt that I was glad differently from the way I would have been, let's say, yesterday or, even more exactly, the day before yesterday.

Then some tool banged against our car's door, and someone, or rather several people, rolled aside the heavy door. First I heard their voices. They spoke German or some closely related language. It sounded as if they were all talking at once. From what I could gather, they wanted us to leave the cars. But instead, it seemed, they squeezed themselves in among us; for a moment I could see nothing. But the news soon spread: suitcases and packages should stay there. Later, they explained, as the words were translated and passed around, later everyone would be given back his belongings, of course. But first disinfecting awaited the luggage, and a bath awaited us. Indeed, it was high time for that, I thought to myself.

Then the natives approached me, and I finally caught my first glimpse of them. I was quite surprised, because, after all, this was the first time in my life that I had set eyes on—at least in such close proximity—real convicts, clad in the striped suits of criminals, with shaven heads and round caps. Naturally I was taken aback a bit by them. Some were answering questions. Others were looking around the boxcars, and still others started moving the packages with the familiarity of porters. And everything was done with a foxlike quickness. On their breasts, next to the customary number for convicts, I also saw a yellow triangle. Fathoming the meaning of the color wasn't difficult, of course. Still, somehow it suddenly caught my eye. During the journey I had almost completely forgotten about that whole business. Their faces, too, were not particularly trustworthy: they had widespread ears, protruding noses, and sunken, cunning, tiny little eyes. Indeed, they looked like Jews in every respect. I found them suspicious and altogether strange.

When they noticed us boys, I saw that they became excited. They began immediately to whisper in a hurried, somewhat frantic manner, and that's when I made the surprising discovery that Jews don't have just one language, namely Hebrew, as I had believed. I slowly gathered that their question was "Reds di jiddis, reds di jiddis, reds di jiddis?" [Do you speak Yiddish?]. The boys and I answered "Nein" [No]. I noticed that this didn't make them particularly happy. Then I could easily tell, because of my knowledge of German, that they were very much interested in our ages. We said: "Vierzehn, fünfzehn" [Fourteen, fifteen], whatever our ages were. They immediately protested with their hands, their heads, their whole bodies: "Zescajn" [Sixteen], they whispered from every direction, "Zescajn." I was astonished, so I asked one of them, "Warum?" [Why?]. "Willst du arbeiten?" [Do you want to work?] he asked me back, with the empty stare of his eyes falling entirely onto mine. I said, "Natürlich" [Naturally], because, on reflection, that's the reason why we had come here, after all. At this he not only grabbed me but also shook my arms with his yellow, bony, hard hands and repeated, "Zescajn . . . verstajszt du? . . . Zescajn!" [Sixteen . . . do you understand? . . . Sixteen!]. I noticed that he was upset. This was very important to him, it seemed, and since we boys had briefly discussed the affair earlier, I yielded, albeit with some humor: "Okay, I'll be sixteen years old." In addition, there were to be no siblings among us, especially no twins, to my great amazement. We should stick to this story regardless of what they said to us and stay completely independent of the truth. But most of all, "Jeder arbeiten, nist ka mide, nist ka krenk" [Everyone works; don't get tired, don't get sick]. This much I learned from them during those two, or perhaps not quite two, minutes that I needed to reach the door from my spot in the boxcar. Then I made a big jump at last, out into the sunshine, into the fresh air.

At first I noticed an expansive lowland area. I was so blinded by this sudden expanse and by the equally white glistening of the sky that it hurt my eyes. But I had little time for gazing around. I was surrounded by hurrying, swarming noises, the broken remnants of words and phrases. Women, I heard, had to say good-bye for a while since, after all, they couldn't bathe with us under the same roof. Old people, weak people, mothers with small children, and also those exhausted by the journey had cars waiting for them further down the road. All of this information was given to us by other prisoners. I noticed, however, that out here German soldiers, with their green caps, green collars, and eloquent hand movements, were pointing out directions, keeping an eye on everything: I was somewhat relieved on seeing them because they seemed well-cared-for, clean, and neat, and in this chaos they alone seemed to exude solidity and calm. I heard the warnings of several grown-ups among us and agreed right away: Let's try to go along, keep good-byes and questions to a minimum. Let's show ourselves intelligent and not set a negative example for the Germans.

I'd have difficulty reporting everything else that followed: the flood of some sort of a porridgy, bubbling maelstrom seized, carried, pushed me along. Behind me a female voice screeched incessantly to someone concerning a certain hand-bag that had come with the woman and was lost. In front of me a decomposed-looking older woman was getting underfoot, and I heard the explanations of a short young man by her: "Listen to them, Mama, since we shall see each other again very soon. Nicht wahr, Herr Offizier?" [Right, Sir Officer?]. He turned familiarly with a typical mature, let's-stick-together smile at a German soldier who happened to be there. "Wir werden uns bald wieder" [We'll soon see each other again]. And then my attention was caught by the terrible screams of a messy, curly-haired little boy dressed like a show-window mannequin as he tried to free himself from the arms of a blond woman, obviously his mother, with strange pulls, twitches, and convulsions. "I want to go with Daddy!" he screamed, shouted, and yelled, stamping his white-shoed feet with ridiculous impatience on the white gravel and the white dust.

In the meantime I also tried to keep up with the boys, to listen to Rozi's occasional calls and directions, while a corpulent woman in a sleeveless, flowery summer dress pushed her way through the crowd, past me, in the direction where we had been notified that cars were waiting. A small, bold gentleman with a black hat and a black tie kept turning around as he was being swept along. With a searching face he scanned the crowd and called out: "Ilonka, my Ilonka." A tall, bony man and a dark-haired woman embraced with their faces, lips, and whole bodies, temporarily annoying everyone. Eventually the woman, or rather the girl, was torn away by the constant battering of the flood of people engulfing her, although in parting I glimpsed her once or twice struggling to rise up and wave good-bye.

All these pictures, sounds, and events confused and dizzied me in this strangely colorful, I would even say crazy, hodgepodge of impressions. Often I was unable to observe the key incidents. And so, for example, I would have difficulty saying who should be credited—us, the soldiers, the convicts, or everyone—for the fact that we finally wound up in a long, regular column, composed entirely of boys and men, with regular lines of five across that moved slowly but steadily forward and in step. Those in the front were measured: I was told that a bath was awaiting us, but first we were to go through a medical examination. They mentioned—and I didn't have any difficulty in understanding, naturally—that there had to be some sort of an inspection concerning our ability for work.

I had time then to catch my breath. We waved and spoke to each other, showing that everything was okay. It was warm. I looked around to orient myself a little as to where we were. The station was neat. Under our feet was the customary crushed stone; a little further away was a border of grass with yellow flowers, and then an immaculate white asphalt road disappeared into infinity. I also noticed that the road was divided from the vastness behind it by a row of identically curved columns with metallically shimmering barbed wire behind them. Guessing was easy: obviously that was where the convicts lived. Only now did they begin to interest me—perhaps because only now did I have the time to think about it—and I was curious to discover what their crimes were.

Distance (that is, the expansiveness of this flat land) surprised me again as I surveyed the surroundings. Surrounded on all sides by this mass of people and in this blinding light, however, I was unable to picture it precisely. I could barely distinguish some distant low-lying buildings and here and there a few hunting-observation perches, towers, and smokestacks. Those around me, boys and grown-ups, were pointing at something up there: a longish, motionless, hard glittering body bored into the cloudless yet still bleached-looking sky's white vapors. It was, indeed, a zeppelin. Most of the people around me explained that it was for air defense; and then once again I remembered the sirens at dawn. Still, I saw no sign of confusion or fear in the German soldiers near us. I remembered the terrified reactions at home to air raids, and this superb calm, this invincibility, suddenly helped me to understand better the respect with which people at home in general spoke of Germans. Just then I noticed two lightning-bolt symbols on their collars. I realized that they must belong to the famous SS troops, of which I had already heard so much back home. I have to admit that I didn't find them the least bit scary: they walked up and down comfortably, circled around the columns, answered questions, nodded, and patted some of us cordially on the backs or shoulders.

I noticed something else as well during the idle minutes of waiting. I had often seen German soldiers at home, naturally. But then they were always in a hurry, with tense, occupied faces and flawless attire. Here, on the other hand, they were different, more relaxed. That was my impression. They moved a bit more casually. I also noticed even smaller differences: softer or stiffer glistening caps, boots, and uniforms, as if made for work. They all wore guns at their sides, and that was quite natural, since, after all, they were soldiers. But in the hands of many I also saw a stick, some kind of hooked walking stick, and that surprised me a little, because, after all, they were obviously men in their prime with steady walks. But then I was able to examine the objects close up. My attention was riveted on a man directly in front of me. With his back half turned, he held his stick almost horizontally behind his hips as, with both hands, he began to bend it with a seemingly bored gesture. My row kept getting closer to him. Only then did I notice that it wasn't made out of wood but of leather, and that it wasn't a walking stick but a whip. I had a strange feeling. But I saw no one trying to use it, and then, I had to admit, there were a lot of convicts around us, after all.

In the meantime I was paying little attention to the announcements. I heard, I remember, that when they called for people with mechanical expertise, some stepped forward. At another time they called for twins, people with physical deformities, and that created some chuckling. They also asked for any dwarfs among us. Then they asked for children, because, as I was told, they were to receive special treatment: study instead of work and a variety of advantages. Some grown-ups in our row urged us not to let this opportunity pass by. But I recalled the warning of the prisoners at the station, and anyway, I felt more like working than living the life of a child, of course.

During all this time we made good progress forward. Then I noticed that suddenly the place was swarming with soldiers and prisoners. Our five-man row had converted into a neat, single-file line. At the same time they ordered us to strip off our coats and shirts, so that we could present ourselves to the doctor bare-chested. The speed, I noticed, was also beginning to increase. At the same time I saw two separate groups up front. A larger group of men and boys was on the right, and a smaller and somehow more appealing group (where I also spotted some of the boys) was on my left. This latter group seemed to contain, so I thought, the more qualified ones. During all of this and with increasing speed, I was heading toward a fixed spot, where, in the middle of this chaos—with a myriad of figures coming and going—I noticed an impeccable uniform with the arched high hat of a German officer. I was surprised at how quickly I had ended up there.

The examination itself only took about two to three seconds. Moskovics was directly ahead of me. He, however, was immediately sent in the opposite direction by the doctor, who just pointed the way with his finger. I heard Moskovics try to explain: "Arbeiten . . . sechzehn" [Work . . . sixteen]. But a hand reached out for him from somewhere, and I immediately took his place. I noticed that I was examined more carefully by the doctor, with serious, attentive, and probing eyes. I stood straight up to show off my chest to him, and I remember that I even smiled a little, right after Moskovics had left. I immediately trusted the doctor, because he was very presentable and had an appealing, longish, clean-shaven face with rather narrow lips, and blue or gray but in any case light and benevolent-looking eyes. I got a good look at him while he, with his gloved hands, pressed against my cheeks and pulled down my lower eyelids with movements that I had already experienced from doctors at home. At the same time he asked me in a quiet yet very clear voice, revealing that he was an educated man: "Wie viel Jahre alt bist du?" [How old are you?]. He asked this almost casually. I replied, "Sechzehn." He nodded lightly but, more to the point, seemed to acknowledge that this was the proper answer. At least that was my impression then. My immediate impression, which may have been a mistaken one, was that he looked somehow satisfied, in a way relieved; I felt that he liked me. And then with one hand still on my cheek and with the other pointing the way, he sent me to the other side, among the qualified ones. The boys were already expecting me triumphantly, laughing with joy. And at the sight of their radiant faces, I perhaps understood the fundamental difference that separated our group from the one across the road: it was success, if I understood it correctly.

Then I put my shirt back on, exchanged a few words with the boys, and again waited. From here I could see what was happening on the other side of the road from a different perspective. A flood of people rolled by in an uninterrupted stream; it was forced into a narrowing riverbed and branched into two rows in front of the doctor. Other boys kept arriving, and now I greeted them, of course. Farther away I noticed another column, that of women. They were surrounded by soldiers and prisoners. In front of them, too, was a doctor; there everything was happening the way it was with us, except that they weren't required to take off their dresses, of course. Everything was working well, everything ran smoothly, everyone was in his place and attended to his function, precisely, cheerfully, like a well-oiled machine. On many faces I saw smiles, rather humble but more self-assured. Some had no doubts, and some anticipated the outcome, but basically they all had the same smile, I suspect, that I felt on my own face.

With that very same smile a brown and, from my vantage point, very beautiful woman, in a white trench coat and round earrings, turned to a soldier with a question. With the very same smile a dark-haired man stepped up in front of the doctor: he was qualified. I quickly enough figured out the doctor's job: old men clearly went to the other side; young men came here with us. Another man with a belly, but standing very straight, was sent in our direction. I wasn't completely happy with this, because, as far as I was concerned, he was over the hill. I also felt compelled to observe that the majority of the men with their unshaven faces made a particularly unfavorable impression. And so I saw with the eyes of the doctor how many old or otherwise unusable men there were here. One was too thin, another too fat; one, because of the constant twitch in his eye and constant movements of his nose and lips, which reminded me of a rabbit, I judged to be mentally ill. Even he, though, knowing his obligations, smiled easily as, with eager ducklike steps, he hurried over to the group of the unqualified. Then there was another case: his coat and shirt were draped over his arm, his suspenders dangled against his thighs, and on his arms and chest some loose skin was beginning to hang. When he reached the doctor—who immediately directed him toward the unqualified group—a new expression appeared on his unshaven face as the peculiar, yet familiar smile died out. His chapped lips stimulated my memory; it seemed as if he had something urgent to say to the doctor. The doctor, however, was no longer looking at him but at the one behind him, and then a hand (presumably the one that had removed Moskovics earlier) pulled him out of the way. He made a move and turned back, with a puzzled and outraged expression on his face: yes, it was the "expert adviser." I don't think I was mistaken.

Then we waited one or two minutes more. In front of the doctor there was still a swarm of people. Here in our group, putting the boys and the men together, there must have been by my estimate about forty of us when they called out: "Let's go for a bath!" A soldier stepped over to us. I couldn't quite tell from where. He was rather short, a bit older, a peaceful-looking man with a large gun. He looked like a common soldier to me. "Los, ge ma rorne!" he said, or something similar—not exactly, I noticed, according to the rules of any grammar. Be that as it may, it sounded very pleasant to my ears, since we boys were getting to be a little impatient, not so much for the soap as for the water, if the truth be told.

A road led through a wire gate into an area past which, it seemed, were the baths. We started in loose groupings, talking, slowly looking around. Behind us the soldier trotted along, totally unmoved. Under our feet, again, was a wide, impeccably kept road. In front of us the whole vast lowland and the sky trembled and shimmered in the heat. I was a little bit concerned. I asked, "Are the baths far away?" As I soon discovered, the baths were only a ten-minute walk from the station. What I saw of the area during this short walk met with my approval, by and large. I was especially excited about a soccer field almost immediately to the right at the first clearing. A green lawn, white gates, white lines necessary for the game—everything was there, inviting, fresh, in good condition and in the best of order. We boys kept saying to ourselves: "After work we'll play ball here."

Even greater joy came with a sight just a few steps further, on the left-hand side of the road: it was water, doubtless a roadside water pump. Directly next to it a red-lettered sign offered us a warning: "Kein Trinkwasser" [Not drinkable]. But at this very moment, naturally, it held none of us back. The soldier was very patient, and I must say, it had been a long time indeed since water tasted this good, even if it did leave a nauseating, sharp chemical aftertaste. Further ahead we saw some houses, the same ones I had already noticed from the station. From close range, though, they looked definitely strange: they were long, flat, of an indeterminable color, with some sort of contraption for ventilation or light extending along their rooftops. Each of them was surrounded by a little patch of red gravel and was separated from the road by a well-cared-for lawn. Between them I noticed, to my amused surprise, little vegetable gardens, cabbage patches, and colorful flower beds. Everything was very clean, neat, and beautiful. Indeed, I had to admit that we were on target back in the brick factory with regard to our decision to come here. Only one thing was missing: some sign of life or movement. But then I thought: "This quiet is probably natural, because, after all, these must be the working hours for the inhabitants."

Turning to the left and passing another barbed-wire fence and another wire gate in one of the courtyards, we reached the bath. I noticed that they were ready for us, and they explained everything courteously. First we entered a kind of anteroom that had a stone floor. There were already several people here whom I recognized from the train. From this I surmised that work here went on uninterruptedly. They must constantly be bringing groups of people over from the station to be bathed. Here a prisoner helped us out. I must say he was an extraordinarily distinguished convict. Although he wore the striped suit of a prisoner, his was equipped with shoulder pads and a tailored coat; I might even say that his garb was cut and ironed in the latest fashion, and besides, he was well combed, with black, shiny hair like us free people. He received us standing at the center of the room's opposite end. To his right, a soldier sat behind a small desk; he was rather small, cheerful, and very fat. His belly began at his neck, and a ruffled double chin surrounded his collar. He had laughing, barely slit eyes in a wrinkled, yellow, hairless face, and he reminded me somehow of the dwarfs they were looking for among us at the station. Still, on his head he wore a hat that commanded respect, and on the table was a shiny, brand-new–looking attaché case with a whip next to it, which was braided with white leather and, I have to admit, beautifully crafted—obviously his personal property.

All of this I was able to observe comfortably, though the spaces between the many heads, while we newcomers tried to fit ourselves into the already filled room. During this time the prisoner hurried back and forth from the opposite end of the room to inform the soldier about something, and with great familiarity he bent himself almost entirely over to the soldier's ear. The soldier seemed satisfied, and I heard his voice, more like that of a child or woman, as he replied with a few sentences. Then the prisoner straightened himself up and, holding up one of his hands, asked us for "peace and quiet." Then I first experienced that often-referred-to feeling of sudden joy upon hearing unexpectedly the familiar sound of a Hungarian word in a foreign country: indeed, I was facing a compatriot. I immediately felt a little sorry for him, because I was forced to see that he was quite young and intelligent, and in spite of his convict status I had to admit that he had a winning face. I greatly desired to find out from where, how, and for what offense he had wound up being a prisoner, but first he simply informed us that he wanted to acquaint us with our new jobs and with the important requests of Herr Oberscharführer. If we complied with all that was asked (which incidentally we most assuredly were expected to do, he added), then everything would go along smoothly and quickly. This, he assured us, was in our self-interest, and this was also the desire of Herr Ober, as he called the soldier, now shortening and abusing the official title in a (at least in my opinion) somewhat too familiar way.

Then he informed us about some simple, and in this case obvious, facts, while the soldier approved of his speech with frequent nods, validating it, because, after all, it was being made by a prisoner. The soldier nodded once to us, once to him, turning his friendly eyes from him to us and back again. We learned, for example, that we were to undress in the next room—that is, in the "dressing room"—and that we were to hang up our clothes neatly on the hangers provided there. These hangers were numbered. While we were bathing, someone would also disinfect our clothes. So it was necessary for him to explain, he said, and I totally agreed with him, that it was important for us not to forget our numbers. I didn't find any difficulty in accepting his useful suggestion that we should tie our shoes together "in order to avoid any potential mix-up," as he put it. Then we would go along to the barbers to be attended to, he promised, and then finally to the baths.

First, however, he said that those who still held on to any money, gold, jewels, or other valuables should step forward and give them voluntarily to Herr Ober for safekeeping, since this was our last opportunity to divest ourselves "without punishment" of our belongings. For, as he explained, all trade, all sorts of selling and buying, and consequently the possession of any valuables or their "transportation" into the camp were "strictly prohibited." He used the expression *camp*, which was new to me but was quite understandable from the German word *Lager*. After the bath, he informed us, they would X-ray all of us with a machine made especially for this purpose. The soldier accompanied his speech with approving nods, noticeably good humor, and unmistakable approval, especially at the word *X-ray*, which obviously pleased him. Then, I remember well, the prisoner said that the guards would have to be duly informed of any smuggling. Of his own free will, he said, he would like to add that any attempt at smuggling would subject the perpetrator to "the most severe penalty," and we would risk the loss of our honor before the German authorities. In his opinion this was all completely "senseless and useless." Without any doubt, I thought he was correct, although the question didn't really concern me. Then near the completion of his speech there was a period of great quiet—a somewhat embarrassing quiet, I felt.

Then there was some movement. Someone asked for some room, stepped forward, placed something on the table, and hurriedly returned to his place. The soldier muttered something to him; it sounded like praise. From my spot I could barely see the object. It was rather small. The soldier immediately dropped it into the drawer of the table. Afterward he glanced at it and quickly assessed it. He struck me as being pleased. Then there was another shorter pause, then again some movement, and another man came forward. And after that and without any pause, men kept stepping forward, more and more courageously and frequently on each other's heels, placing shiny or metallically clicking objects onto the small empty space between the whip and the attaché case. All this— excluding the sound of steps, objects hitting the table, and the responding short, thin, but always good-humored and encouraging remarks of the soldier—happened in complete silence. I also noticed that the soldier used precisely the same procedure with each object. Even if someone placed two objects in front of him, he still examined them individually—sometimes nodding approvingly—first one, then the other. Then he pulled open the drawer, placed each object inside, and closed the drawer again, usually with his stomach, so that he could return to the next object and repeat the procedure. I was quite surprised how much turned up this way, even after the experience in Hungary. And I was equally surprised by the hurry and the sudden eagerness of people, since until now they had been willing to accept any kind of trouble and danger associated with the possession of such objects. That is probably why I noticed the same expressions on the faces of those returning from the table: a little embarrassed, a little solemn, but certainly somewhat relieved. After all, we were standing at the gates of a new life here, and I could see that this was an altogether different situation than back at the barracks. All this took about three or four minutes, I would guess.

I can't say very much about anything else: basically everything happened according to the prisoner's instructions. The opposite door opened, and we entered a room that was furnished with long benches and clothes hangers. I immediately found a number and repeated it several times to myself so that I wouldn't forget it. I also tied my shoes together, just as the prisoner had suggested. Then we went into a large, brightly lit room with a low ceiling. All around the walls razors worked and electric haircutters hummed; the barbers, all convicts, were hard at work. I got one on the right side. "Sit down," he presumably said, since I didn't understand his language, and I sat on the stool in front of him. Soon he was pressing the machine against my neck and shaving off my hair, down to the last follicle, so that I was totally bald. Then he took a razor and shaved me. I had to stand up and raise my arm, and then he scratched under my arm with the razor. Then he sat down in front of me and grabbed me by that organ that is most sensitive and with his razor scraped away the whole crown, every single hair, every tiny bit of male pride that only recently started to sprout. Probably very stupidly, I felt this last loss even more acutely than the loss of my upper hair. I was astonished and somewhat angry, but I realized that it would be ridiculous to get all upset about such a trifle. And besides, I noticed that everyone else, including the boys, fared likewise, and we said right away to Silky Boy: "Well, well, what are you going to do with the girls now?"

But then they shouted: "The baths are waiting." In the doorway a prisoner pressed a small piece of soap into the hand of

Rozi, who was in front of me, and signaled that this had to be enough for three of us. In the baths we found slippery wooden planks under our feet and a network of pipes with a tremendous number of shower heads above us. There were soon plenty of naked and not particularly pleasant-smelling people there. Very interesting was the fact that the water started flowing all by itself, quite unexpectedly, after everyone, including myself, had been searching for the knobs to turn it on. The water pressure wasn't particularly strong, but I found the temperature refreshingly cool and in this heat quite pleasing.

First I had a drink, and I encountered the same taste as at the fountain. Only after relieving my thirst did I enjoy the feel of water on my skin. Round about me were cheerful noises—splashing, sneezing, blowing. This was a humorous, carefree moment as we boys kept teasing each other about our bald heads. We found out that the soap didn't lather up but contained lots of scratchy particles. Still, nearby was a round man with curly black hair on his chest (which, it seems, was untouched by the razor), who was soaping himself up with solemn (I would say almost ceremonious) movements. Something, aside from the hair on his head, also seemed missing as I looked at him. Only then did I notice that the skin on his chin and face was whiter than elsewhere and was full of fresh red cuts. It was the rabbi from the brick factory. I recognized him now. So he too had come. Minus his beard, he looked far less unusual: now he was a simple, somewhat large-nosed but basically pedestrian-looking man. He was in the process of scrubbing his legs when—with the same suddenness with which it had begun—the water stopped. The rabbi looked up, surprised, then again looked back down in front of him, but somehow in an accepting way, just as someone accepts, understands, and at the same time bows down before the power of a higher decree.

I could do nothing else either: they were already carrying me, pushing me out of the room. We reached a poorly lit place where a prisoner pressed a handkerchief—no, as it turned out, a towel—into everyone's hands, including mine. He motioned that I should return it after I was done. Then another prisoner brushed some suspiciously colored, itchy disinfecting fluid (judging by its incredibly nose-twitching smell) under my arms and also on that especially sensitive area with a flat kind of a brush and with an unexpected, extremely quick, and clever move. Then a hallway followed, lighted on the right by two windows, and finally a third doorless room: in each room stood a prisoner handing out clothes. Just like all the others I received a shirt that had once had blue and white stripes; it was cut like those in my grandfather's time, without a collar or buttons at the neck. I also got pants suitable for old men, slit at the ankles and tied with two strings at the bottom, as was done ages ago. It was a well-worn outfit, the exact replica of the kind worn by convicts, made of canvas with blue and white stripes—a real convict's suit, no matter how I looked at it. Then in the open room I was able to choose from a mountain of strange, wooden-soled, canvas-inlaid shoes, not tied by shoe strings but fastened on the sides with three buttons. I grabbed what seemed to be a pair nearly my size. And let me not forget two gray pieces of cloth, intended, I thought, as handkerchiefs. Then, finally, I realized that they were the inevitable soft, round, worn-out, cross-striped convict's cap. I hesitated a little, but from all sides voices hurried me on, and in the feverish grabbing and the fast dressing around me I couldn't take my time if I didn't want to be left behind by the others. Since the pants were wide and were missing a belt or some sort of suspender, I was forced to tie them in a knot, and that on the run. I also discovered an unanticipated quality about the shoes: their soles didn't bend. During all this time, in order to keep my hands free, I placed the cap on my head. The other boys were ready too. We kept looking at each other, not knowing whether to laugh or look astonished. But there was no time for either. We were already outside again in the fresh air. I don't know who made the arrangements, nor do I know what happened exactly: I only remember that some pressure descended on me, some movement began, pushing me forward in my new shoes, in the middle of a cloud of dust and with strange puffs from behind that sounded as if someone's back was perhaps being whipped, impelling me forward through new yards, new wire gates, new barbed wires, through an opening that closed and that finally led us chaotically to a tangled network of fences.

5

There is no new prisoner, I think, who is not a little bewildered at first by his situation. So, on arriving at the courtyard from the baths, we boys stared at one another for a long time, turning one another around and staring in wonder. Then a young-looking man who was nearby caught my attention. For a long time and with great concentration, but at the same time hesitatingly, he kept touching his clothes as if he was trying to convince himself of the true quality of the material. Then he looked up, like someone who suddenly has something to say but on seeing nothing except the same clothing around him decides to say nothing. At least that was my impression at that moment. Of course, I was probably mistaken. I recognized him, in spite of his boldness and the convict suit that was too short for his height, because of his bony face: he was the man in love who about an hour before—the time between our arrival and our metamorphosis—had had such a difficult time letting go of the dark-haired girl.

One thing I now greatly regretted: At home I had once taken down a book from the shelf, a hidden book that had been collecting dust there for who knows how long. Its author was a prisoner. I didn't finish reading it because I couldn't follow his train of thought, and also because the characters had tremendously long and impossible-to-remember names, and, finally, because I wasn't the least bit interested in and, to be quite honest, was somewhat disgusted by the lives of the prisoners. And so I was now unprepared in my time of need. From the whole book I could only remember one thing: the author insisted that he remembered the first days of his captivity—that is, those farthest from the time of the composition—better than the later days that were closer to him. I thought then that such a statement was doubtful, somewhat exaggerated. Yet I now believe that he must have been correct. For I myself can now remember my first day most precisely, indeed, more exactly, when I think of it than all the ones that followed.

At first I felt myself, so to speak, like a guest in the world of convicts—not just me, but all of us—I believe because of the understandably deceptive tendencies of human nature. The yard, that sun-beaten place, seemed a bit bare. I saw no trace of a soccer field or a vegetable garden or a lawn or flowers. Only an unadorned, barnlike wooden building stood here—obviously our home to be. I was told we'd only be able to enter it at night. In front of and behind it were long rows of similar barns extending into infinity; to the left was another such row with spaces at regular intervals. Beyond that was a wide, glistening main road—or some other road, since after returning from the baths the sameness of the roads, courtyards, and buildings on this homogeneous, flat surface made any orientation impossible, at least to my eyes. At the spot where this main road intersected with the crossroads between the barns, passage was blocked by a toylike, very pretty red and white slender gate. To the right stood the familiar barbed-wire fence, which, I was surprised to learn, was electrified. Indeed, only then did I did recognize that the many white porcelain knobs on its concrete columns were similar to those at home on electric wires and telegraph posts. Its striking power, they assured us, was deadly. Furthermore, stepping on the narrow path of loose sand in front of it was sufficient for us to be shot without warning from the guard tower (which I had earlier thought was a hunting tower). Then we were warned about everything around there by those who were informed.

Soon some volunteer prisoners arrived, with a lot of noise and banging, weighed down by some heavy brick-red pots. A little while before, the news had quickly spread through the whole courtyard that we were soon to receive some hot soup! Needless to say, I found this news interesting, but still I was somewhat puzzled by those radiant faces, that gratitude, that peculiar, almost childlike joy with which so many received it. Maybe that is why I felt that their reaction was not so much to the soup but to the care itself, especially after all those previous surprises. At least that was my conjecture. I also thought that the news probably stemmed from that prisoner who suddenly seemed to be our guide, our host, so to speak, in this place. He too, like the prisoner in the baths, wore tailored clothes, and he had hair that seemed unusual to me, with a dark-blue cap covering it, known at home as a Basque cap. On his feet were some good-looking yellow shoes, and on his arm a red ribbon immediately announced his authority. I at once saw that I'd have to revise, it seemed, a concept that they had taught me at home, according to which clothes don't make the man. He also wore a red triangle on his chest; that too immediately showed everyone that he was here not because of his blood, but merely because of his philosophy, as I soon discovered. With us he was friendly, albeit measured and somewhat brief, but he explained the rules very readily, and I saw nothing unusual in that, since after all he had been living here much longer than we had. He was tall, rather thin, a little worn-looking, but all in all a quite likable man. I also noticed that he often stood to the side. I spotted him looking at us once or twice with a puzzled, un-comprehending expression and with a certain (how shall I say it?) head-shaking-in-disapproval smile at the corners of his lips, as if he was somewhat amazed at us. I'm not sure why. Later they said he was of Slovak descent. Some among us newcomers spoke his language and formed small groups around him.

He doled out the soup to us with a strange, long serving spoon that had something of a funnel shape. There were two other assistants who similarly were different from us, and they offered us red tin plates and beaten-up spoons—one for every two of us because supplies were low, they informed us. For the same reason, they added, we had to return the utensils as soon as we were finished. After a while I finally had my turn. I took the soup, plate, and spoon, sharing them with Leather-Worker. I wasn't especially happy, because I had never had the habit of eating with others from the same plate and with the same spoon, but necessity, I admitted to myself, might occasionally dictate this too. Leather-Worker first tasted the soup and then quickly gave it to me. His face looked strange. I asked him what it was; he answered that I should try it for myself. By then I saw that all of the boys were looking at one another, some shocked, some bursting with laughter. Then I also tasted the soup and had to admit that it was inedible. I asked Leather-Worker what we should do, and he replied that, as far as he was concerned, I was welcome to pour it all out. At the same time a cheerful voice behind me offered an explanation: "This is called Dörgemüze," he explained. He was a stocky, mature-looking man, with a white spot under his nose taking the place of a square mustache; his face was brimming with well-intentioned knowledge. To the frowning men milling around us, holding their plates and spoons in their hands, he explained that he had taken part in the earlier war, that is, the First World War, as an officer. Then he had had ample opportunity, he said, "to become thoroughly knowledgeable about this food" with his fellow German soldiers at the front, with whom he had lived in a camp. According to him this was nothing but dried vegetables. "For a Hungarian stomach," he added with an understanding and somewhat forgiving smile, "it is, of course, unusual." But he insisted that one could, or even should, get used to this soup, because "it is very nutritious and full of vitamins," which attested to the Germans' expertise in these matters. "Besides," he noted with another smile, "the first rule of a good soldier is to eat everything that you get today, because you don't know if you'll get anything tomorrow." Those were his words.

And then, indeed, he spooned up his portion peacefully, steadily, without a single frown, until the last drop. Still, I poured mine against the corner of the barracks in the same way that I had seen some grown-ups and other boys do. I was embarrassed, because I noticed the glance of our foreman from afar, and I was worried that he might be hurt by this; but all that I could detect, and that only hurriedly, was that same odd expression, that somewhat indefinable smile on his face. Then I returned the plate and received a large piece of bread shaped like a building block with some white substance on top. This was not butter, but margarine, so they said. This I ate, even though I had never seen bread to equal it: it was big and crusty, and its insides seemed to be baked with black mud full of straw and kernels that kept crunching under my teeth. Still, it was bread, and the long trip had made me famished. For lack of a better utensil, I spread the margarine with my finger, in Robinson Crusoe fashion, so to speak, in the same way that the others did. Then I looked around for some water, but unfortunately there was none. I was quite annoyed. We would be thirsty again, just like on the train.

At this point we finally had to pay some serious attention to a smell. It was difficult for me to determine whether it was sweet or sticky, mixed in as it was with that already familiar chemical scent, but this new odor was so powerful that I feared that the bread that I had just eaten was going to come back up in my throat. The smell was not hard to locate. On the left toward the road but farther away than that was a chimney, which was the cause. It was a factory chimney, we soon learned from our foreman. To be more precise, it was the chimney of a leather factory, as many later told us. Indeed, I recall going with Father occasionally to an Újpest soccer game on Sundays; the streetcar passed by a leather factory, and for that stretch of the journey I always had to hold my nose. But anyway, so went the news, we would fortunately not have to work in that factory. If everything went well, if there was no typhoid, dysentery, or other epidemic, we would soon, we were assured, move on to a friendlier place. This is the reason why we still had no numbers on our clothes or, more important, on our skins as, for example, our "block commander" did. They now referred to our leader by that title. Several people, by the way, proved to themselves the existence of this number with their own eyes. It was written in green ink—so the news spread—on the block commander's wrist. It had been tattooed, injected with a needle and indelible ink.

About the same time I also heard a story about those who had volunteered to bring in the soup. They too saw numbers on the skins of the prisoners working in the kitchen. They passed on this word and tried to explore the meaning, as they repeated the news frequently. One of the prisoners supposedly answered the question about this number's purpose this way: "Himmlische Telefonnummer" [heavenly telephone number]. I noticed that the incident made everyone think, and while I couldn't make heads or tails of it myself, without a doubt I also found all this very strange.

At any rate, it was then that people started coming and going, attacking the block commander and his assistant with questions, exchanging the information received quickly among themselves. For example, they asked, "Is there an epidemic here?" "Yes" was the answer. "What happens to the sick people?" "They die." "What happens to the dead?" "They are burnt." In truth, it gradually became clear (I don't quite know when) that the chimney opposite us was not really on a leather factory but a crematorium. It was the chimney of a cremating establishment, as they explained it to me. Then I looked more closely: it was a thick, square, wide-mouthed chimney built as if someone had chopped off its top. I can say that, aside from a certain respect and, of course, the smell, with which we were stuck as if we were in a thick stew or a swamp, I felt nothing. But in the distance we noticed one, then another, and then at the edge of the radiant sky still another chimney, to our great surprise. These poured forth smoke just like ours. Some people suspected that the smoke coming from behind a wild arbor far away was the same kind. They wondered (and I thought rightly): Is the epidemic really so great that there are this many dead?

6

I can say with confidence that the first day didn't come to a close without my getting a clear view of everything, by and large. Admittedly, we first visited the toilet facilities several times. It consisted of three platformlike constructions on which there were two rows of holes—six in all—and over these one had to squat or aim, depending on one's need. At any rate, there was not much time for either, because very soon an angry prisoner guard made his appearance—with a black arm ribbon and with a heavy-looking club in his hand—and one had to leave in whatever condition one was in. Some other old-timers were also hanging around; they were much nicer and were quite willing to answer our questions.

To get to the latrine and back, we had to walk quite a distance under the instruction of the block commander. The road led along some interesting settlements. Behind the wire fence were the usual barns, and among them were some strange women (one I immediately turned my back on, because something was hanging out of her dress and a bold-faced baby clung tenaciously to it while the sun reflected from his skull) and some even stranger men, wearing much-used clothes, but still of the kind worn outside, in the free life, so to speak. Coming back, I learned that this was a gypsy camp. I was a little surprised. At home everybody had some reservations about the gypsies, myself included, but until now I hadn't heard that they too were sinners. Then a cart arrived, which was pulled by small children with reins over their shoulders, as if they were ponies; next to them walked a man with a big mustache and a whip in his hand. The contents of the cart were covered with blankets, but through the many holes and openings I caught a glimpse of bread, of white loaves, unmistakably. From that I concluded that they had to stand a notch above us.

Another sight during that walk stuck in my mind: in the other direction on the main road walked a man who looked left and right and wore a white suit with a wide red border on his white pants and a large black artist's cap like those that, according to pictures, medieval painters used to wear. He held a thick gentleman's walking stick in his hand. I had a very hard time believing—as I was told—that this majestic man was, after all, a prisoner just like the rest of us.

I can swear one thing: I personally did not speak to any strangers on this road. Still, my more precise knowledge of affairs stems from this time. There across the way our fellow travelers were being burnt—all those who had asked to be transported by car, all those who had been judged "unqualified" by the doctor because of age or any other reason, all the children with their mothers, as well as any expecting mothers who, as they said, were "showing it." From the station they had also gone to the baths. They too were informed about the hangers and the numbers, and the whole procedure was just like ours. They also saw the barbers, I was told, and they also received a piece of soap. Then they also reached the showers, where I heard that there were the same pipes and shower heads, yet it wasn't water but gas that poured down on them. All this I didn't learn at once, but bit by bit, with the constant addition of new details, some questioned, some reaffirmed, some elaborated upon.

I also heard that during all this process, they were treated cordially, were even surrounded by care and affection. The children played ball and sang, and the place where they suffocated to death was surrounded by beautiful lawns, arbors, and flower beds. That is the reason why all that somehow reminded me of a student's practical joke. Besides, this impression was reinforced when I remembered how cleverly they had got me undressed and redressed with the simple idea of the hangers and the numbers and how they had scared everyone who possessed valuables with the notion of an X-ray machine, which finally turned out to be nothing more than a threat. Of course, I realized that this was really no joke, if I looked at it closely, because I was aware of its results from what I saw later and by the way my stomach behaved; but this was my initial reaction, and basically—at least that is how I imagined things happened—it probably was planned in the same way that a practical joke is planned. After all, they probably got together, probably stuck their heads together even if they weren't students, of course, but established grown-ups, perhaps, or, more probably, or even more certainly when I think about it, gentlemen in respectable suits, with cigars, and with medals on their breasts—all leaders, presumably, who could not be disturbed, as I pictured them. One of them had dreamed up the gas, another the baths, still another the soap. A fourth added the flowers, and so on it went. They probably debated one or another idea at length to try to improve upon it, while other ideas suddenly appealed to them, and they jumped up (I don't know why, but I insisted on the fact that they jumped up) and slapped each other's hands in congratulation. All of this was easy to imagine, at least for me. The commanders' imagination was then put into reality by busy, active hands, and there could be no question, I have to admit, concerning the success of the execution.

This was the end, doubtless, of the old woman who had been talking to her son, the little boy with the white shoes and his blond mother, the fat woman, the old gentleman with the black hat, and the mentally ill man in front of the doctor. I remembered the "expert adviser" too; I'm sure he must have been astonished, poor soul. Rozi also shook his head sympathetically and said, "Poor Moskovics," and we all had the same opinion. Silky Boy also cried out, "Jesus!" He confessed to us the truth about him and the girl at the brick factory; "everything" indeed had taken place, as the boys suspected, and now he was thinking of the eventual results of his deed, which would soon be visible on her. We admitted that his concern was justified, although besides this concern there seemed to be another, difficult-to-define emotion on his face. The boys were looking at him with a kind of respect at that moment. I, of course, didn't find that the least bit difficult to understand. Another thing gave me pause for reflection that day: this institution had been here for years, I learned, standing right here, functioning the same way every day—as if it had been waiting explicitly for me. I realized that there was some exaggeration in this thought, but still, it struck me that way. At any rate, as several people mentioned with a strange, frightening respect, our block commander had been living here for four years already. Then I remembered that that year (four years ago) was a very important one for me, too, because I had registered for high school then. I remembered the induction ceremonies clearly: I was there in a dark-blue Hungarian suit, called a Bocskai habit. I remembered the words of the head-master—a respectable man, now that I think of it, somewhat like a commander, with strict-looking glasses and a handsome white mustache. I recall his quoting an ancient philosopher at the close of his speech: "Non scolae sed vitae discimus"; "We learn not for the school but for life." But I think that we should have been studying about Auschwitz all along, if they had tried to explain everything openly, honestly, intelligently. During the four years at school I did not hear a single word about this place. Still, of course, I realized that it would have been embarrassing, and I guess it really wasn't part of our general education.

The disadvantage was that I had to learn here on my own that we were in a "concentration camp," a *Konzentrationslager*. Even these places weren't all the same, I was informed. This concentration camp, for example, was a *Vernichtungslager*, that is, an "annihilation camp." An *Arbeitslager*, "labor camp," was an entirely different place: there life was easy; the circumstances and the food, they said, were not comparable, which is natural, because, after all, that camp's purpose was different. We were supposed to go to such a place, provided nothing happened to prevent us; this, several people admitted, could conceivably happen. At any rate, we were warned that it was not advisable to report in sick, since the camp hospital was at the foot of one of the chimneys, called by the initiated by the abbreviated name "Number 2." We ran the greatest danger with water, unboiled water, that is, like the water I had drunk on the way from the station to the baths—but after all I couldn't have known this. Admittedly there had been a sign. I can't deny that, but still, I thought, the soldier should have said something to me. But wait, I said to myself. I should look at the fundamental purpose of the camp, shouldn't I? Still, fortunately, I felt fine, and I didn't hear any complaints from the other boys either.

Later that day I acquainted myself with other information about sights and customs. I have to say that in the afternoon I heard some more news: there was more talk of our future prospects, possibilities, and hopes than of the chimneys. At those times it was as if they weren't there. We paid no attention to them. It all depended on the way the wind blew, as many admitted. That same day I saw some women too, for the first time. They were pointed out by an excited group of men at the wire fence: there they were, indeed, although I found it difficult to recognize them (even as women) because they were far away, on the other side of the playing fields. I was a little scared by then, and I noticed that the other men and boys, too, had quieted down a bit after the first joy, the excitement of discovery. Only a muted, somewhat shaky remark reached my ears: "They are bold." And in this great quiet, I first perceived the thin, interrupted, barely audible, yet undoubtedly real sound of peaceful, cheerful music carried on the wings of the light summer breeze. Together with the sight before us, this surprised us all tremendously. Similarly, for the first time I stood waiting in front of our barracks (as I found out later) in one of the last of the ten-man rows just like all the other prisoners in front of all the other barracks, to the side, to the front, to the back, wherever I looked. And for the first time I pulled off my cap, as I was told to do. Suddenly out there on the main road the figures of three soldiers on bicycles became visible, gliding along calmly and quietly in the soft evening air. It was a beautiful sight—I had to admit—and a solemn one, actually.

Then I remembered: it had been some time since we had seen any soldiers. I was perplexed how these three men, so rigidly, so ice-coldly, as if from an unreachable height, listened (as one of them made notes in a thick notebook) to the report of our block commander from the other side of the gate (he too held his cap in his hand) and then without a single word, a sound, or even a nod of the head glided further down the empty main road. I wondered how these ominous beings of might and power could be members of the same friendly, cheerful group that had met us at the train. At the same time a quiet voice reached my ears, and to my right I saw a raised profile and the curve of a chest: it was the former military officer. He whispered, barely moving his lips: "Evening mustering." He nodded briefly with the smile and the informed face of a person for whom everything is clear, understandable, and to a certain degree almost to his liking. And then as night fell, I studied the color of the sky and saw one of its marvels: Greek fire, a virtual fireworks of sparkles and flames on the left horizon. "Crematoriums," people whispered, mumbled, repeated around me, but now only with a kind of admiration for natural occurrences. Then came the order to *abtreten* (dissolve the rows). I was quite hungry, but as it happened, one piece of bread was to be our whole supper, and I had eaten that already in the morning. We then found our barracks. The "block" was entirely bare on the inside; it was a room without any furniture and even without lights, with concrete floors where the night's rest had to be arranged the same way as it was in the horse stables at the barracks. I leaned my back against the legs of a boy behind me and supported the back of the boy in front of me with my knees. Since I was tired after all these new experiences and impressions, I quickly fell asleep.

I remember far fewer details from the subsequent days. Just as in the brick factory, only a general feeling or impression remained. Defining it would be difficult. During these days there was much to be learned, seen, and experienced. Once or twice during these days I was touched by the cold of that same strange, peculiar feeling that I felt when I first saw the women. It also happened once or twice when I found myself in a ring of shocked, incredulous faces staring at one another repeating: "What do you say to that? What do you say to that?" And the answer in these situations was either nothing or always the same: "Terrible." But that is not the word, that is not exactly the term I would use to characterize Auschwitz, speaking entirely for myself, naturally.

Among the several hundred inhabitants of our block was also the man with the bad luck, as it turned out. He looked strange in his loose convict's suit and his wide cap that constantly slipped down over his forehead. "What do you say to that? What do you say to that?" he too kept saying. But what could we say, indeed? I couldn't follow his confused, hurried words very well. One should not think, or rather one should think of one thing only: those he "left at home," for whose sake "he had to be strong" because they expected him back. He has to think about his wife and his two small children. This was the gist of it, from what I could gather. The main problem, though, here as well as in the customhouse, the train, and the brick factory, was the length of the days. They began very early, barely after the midsummer sunrise. That was the time when I found out how cold the Auschwitz mornings were. We boys squatted against the barracks on the side facing the wire fence, close to one another, trying to keep one another warm, exactly opposite from the red sun rising at an angle. A few hours later, on the other hand, we would be looking for shade. At any rate, here too time passed; here too we had Leather-Worker with us; here too a few jokes were cracked. Here too we played, if not with horseshoe nails, then with stones that were all won by Silky Boy; here too Rozi occasionally called out, "Let's sing it in Japanese now!"

In addition, we took two walks daily to the latrine, and in the morning also to the wash-up barracks (similar to the latrine, except that instead of the platforms, there were three rows of troughs with parallel pipes over them through whose close-cut holes water trickled). The distribution of food, the mustering in the evening, and, of course, the information-passing—I had to make do with all this because it was the order of the day. Add to this the "events": For example, there was a *Blocksperre*, "block closing," on the second evening; then for the first time I saw our commander impatient, even annoyed, I would say. Also, various noises filtered into the somewhat heavy darkness of the barracks, and if we listened carefully, we thought we could distinguish screams, the barking of dogs, shots. Another time we saw a march, again behind the wire fence, of those returning from work, so some said, but I had to believe that some dead people were lying on those contraptions that were carried by the men in the back, just the way people around me claimed. All of this naturally kept my imagination occupied for a while, but it wasn't quite enough to fill the long idle days. This is when I found out that you could be bored even in Auschwitz—provided you were choosy. We waited and we waited, and as I come to think of it, we waited for nothing to happen. This boredom, combined with this strange waiting, was, I think, approximately what Auschwitz meant to me, but of course I am only speaking for myself.

I have to admit one thing: on the second day I ate my soup, and on the third day I was even anticipating it. In general I found the timing of the meals in Auschwitz rather strange. Early in the morning a certain fluid arrived: coffee, they said. Then they served the soup—that is to say, lunch—surprisingly early, around nine usually. But then nothing happened until the bread with the margarine arrived in the hour before the mustering. And so by the third day I made an acquaintance with the annoying sense of hunger, and the other boys were also complaining about this. Only Smoker observed that, as far as he was concerned, the feeling was nothing new, and he just missed his cigarettes. Aside from his customary short, strange way of speaking, there was an almost satisfied expression on his face, which annoyed me a little, and the other boys also, I think, criticized him for this reason.

Regardless of how surprised I was, regardless of how I counted, the fact was that I spent only three full days in Auschwitz altogether. On the fourth evening I was once again sitting in a train, in one of those already-familiar freight cars. The destination, we were told, was Buchenwald, and even though I was now more careful with such promising names, I felt I perceived a certain tender, nostalgic, somewhat envious expression on the faces of some of the other prisoners at the friendliness (I would almost say the unmistakable implication of warmth) of the name as they were saying good-bye to us. I felt I couldn't be entirely mistaken. I had to notice that there were many old-timers among our well-wishers who knew a lot, several higher-level ones distinguished by armbands, shoes, and caps. At the train they made all the arrangements. I saw only a few soldiers, mostly of low rank, further away by the ramp, and at this quiet spot, in the gentle colors of this peaceful evening, nothing, except perhaps the largeness of the place, reminded me of that hustling and bustling, noisy, teeming, and everywhere vibrating station where we once—or more precisely, three days before—had gotten off the train.

I can say even less about this trip now: everything happened as usual. We were not sixty but eighty in a car, although we had no luggage and we didn't have to make special arrangements for women. Here too there was a pot; here too we were hot; here too we were thirsty. But here there were fewer temptations in the way of food: our rations—a larger-than-usual slab of bread, with a double portion of margarine and something else, some so-called wurst that at least externally reminded me of thick sausages from home—were doled out at the station. I ate them all up right then and there, first, because I was hungry; second, because there was no place on the train to store them; and finally, because they didn't tell us at this time that the journey would take three days.

We arrived in Buchenwald in the morning, on a sunny day cooled by a light, fresh breeze. The station here, at least when compared with Auschwitz, seemed rather provincial and quite friendly. But our reception was less friendly. Here soldiers, not prisoners, pulled open the doors. Actually, I realized that this was really the first occasion I had had to—how shall I say it?—be in close contact with them. I studied the speed and exactness with which everything was accomplished. A few short shouts: "Alle raus!" "Los!" "Fünf Reihen!" "Bewegt euch!" [Everyone out! Away! Five Rows! Move!], a few thumps, a few cracks, the swing of a boot here and there, the thrust of a gun once or twice, a few muted screams—and we were already marching as if pulled by strings and in perfect formation, joined at the end of the platform on each side by a soldier placed at every five rows a half step away. That is, they were joining every twenty-fifth stripe-suited man at a distance of approximately one meter.

Never for a second taking their eyes off the marching column, the soldiers silently controlled the speed and direction with their steps, and as we were led in this way, the column reminded me of caterpillars of my childhood that were nudged along in a matchbox with pieces of paper, moving in waves just the way our column moved forward. I was in some ways mesmerized, fascinated by it all. I had to smile a little when I remembered the policemen's nonchalant, almost modest accompaniment at home on that day as we were going to the barracks. But the behavior of the military policemen, I had to admit, seemed only noisily self-important compared with this silent and in every respect harmonized professionalism. And although I could see their faces well, the color of their eyes or hair, one or another characteristic distinction, or even some flaws, a pimple or a bump on their skins, still I was not able to grasp all of this. I almost had to doubt it. Really, in spite of everything, were these people who were marching beside us basically the same as us? Were they made of roughly the same human materials that we were? But I thought that my way of looking at this was probably flawed, because I was not the same as they were, of course.

I noticed that we were climbing a road leading up at varying degrees of steepness. Again, this was an excellent road, but, unlike the straight one in Auschwitz, undulating. I saw a lot of natural greenery along the sides and some nice-looking ordinary buildings, and further away country villas nestled among trees, parks, and gardens; the whole place seemed normal, I dare say even pleasant, at least to an eye accustomed to Auschwitz. On the right-hand side of the road I was surprised by a little zoo inhabited by deer, rodents, and other animals, including a warm-furred bear, who excitedly assumed a begging position as soon as he heard our steps and performed some clownish movements in his cage. This time his efforts went unrewarded, naturally.

Then we passed a statue that stood on a clean square dividing the road into two forks. Made of white dull stone, standing on a white platform of the same stone, it had been executed, in my opinion, with somewhat rough, careless artistry. Clearly the striped attire, the bold head, and most of all the pose depicted a prisoner. His head leaned forward, and with one of his legs behind him, pushing upward in the air, he was imitating a running step, while in his lap his two hands were entwined tightly around an incredibly large piece of stone. At first I only looked at it like a connoisseur, so to speak—the way I was taught at school—without any further motives. Only later did it occur to me that this statue had a meaning that couldn't be viewed as particularly favorable, if you thought about it. But then my eyes were greeted by some thickly woven wire fences and an open, ornate iron gate with glass above it, which reminded me somehow of the commanding bridge on a ship, surrounded by thick stone columns. Shortly I was passing through this gate. I had arrived at the Buchenwald concentration camp.

7

Buchenwald lies in a mountainous region at the crest of a hill. Its air is clean. In the camp one's eyes were delighted by various views: forests were all around, and the red roofs of village houses lay in the valley below. The baths here were to the left. The prisoners, by and large, were friendly, although different from the ones in Auschwitz. After arriving, one was met here too by a bath, barbers, disinfectants, and a change of clothes. The inventory of the wardrobe was the same as in Auschwitz, but the bath was warmer, the barbers performed their tasks more carefully, and the wardrobe keeper tried, even if only in passing, to hand out clothes that were approximately the right size.

Then you approached a hallway facing a sliding glass door, where they asked you if by chance you had any gold teeth. Then a compatriot of yours with hair, who had lived here longer, wrote your name down in a large book and handed you a yellow triangle, a thick stripe, and a ribbon, all made of canvas. In the center of the triangle, which signified that you were Hungarian, was a large letter U, and on the stripe you could read a printed number; mine, for example, was 64921. It was advisable, I was told, to learn the number's pronunciation in German and to pronounce it clearly this way: "Vierund-sechzig, neun, einundzwanzig." From that time on that was to be my answer if anyone asked for my identification. But your number was not inscribed on your skin, and if you were worried about it and you asked around in the baths or their environs, an old prisoner would protest with raised arms, turning his eyes toward heaven: "Aber, Mensch, um Gottes Willen! Wir sind doch ja hier nicht in Auschwitz" [But man, for God's sake! We are after all not in Auschwitz here]. In addition, the number as well as the triangle had to be sewn on your clothes by that evening, and this was done with the help of the sole proprietors of needle and thread, namely the tailors. If you got tired of standing in line until sunset, you could inspire these men by the promise of a certain portion of your bread and margarine allotment, but they were happy to do it anyway, they said, because, after all, that was their job.

Buchenwald's weather was cooler than Auschwitz's. The days were gray, and there was a frequent drizzle. But it happened sometimes in Buchenwald that one was surprised at breakfast with hot soup. Here I learned that the bread allotment was one-third of the usual portion and on certain days even one-half, not as in Auschwitz where it was usually one-fourth and occasionally one-fifth. In the thickness of the noonday soup one could find some red threads of meat and in some fortunate cases even a whole chunk. In addition, it was here that I made my acquaintance with the concept of a *Zulage* [supplement], which took the form of an additional piece of sausage or a spoonful of jam added to the usual margarine. The officer present would look very pleased then.

In Buchenwald we lived in camps, in a *Zeltlager* [tent camp] or, by another name, *Kleinlager* [little camp], and we slept on bunks strewn with straw. Even though our sleeping places were not separated and were somewhat close to each other, we slept horizontally. The wire fence here was not electrified in the back, but those who, God forgive them, stepped out of the tent at night were torn apart by dogs—so they warned us. Even if you were surprised by the warning, you didn't ever doubt its seriousness. By the other fence, however, where the large part of the actual camp spread its cobblestone street on the hillside and where neat green barracks and little one-storied stone houses started, there were bargains to be found every evening: sales by the old-time prisoners of spoons, knives, food containers, and clothing. One of them offered me a sweater in exchange for just half a piece of bread—he showed me this by signals—but I didn't buy it from him, because in the summer I didn't need a sweater, and the winter, I thought, was still a long way off. Then I also noticed how many varieties of colored triangles there were and how many different letters they contained. I could make neither heads nor tails of them: Who was finally from which country?

But around here I also heard quite a few country-colored expressions and also that strange language that I had first heard spoken by the prisoners who had received us in Auschwitz. In Buchenwald there was no mustering for the inhabitants of the tent camp, and the bath was under the sky, or rather under shady trees. It was constructed in the same way as at Auschwitz, except that the trough was made of stone and, more important, water flowed, spurted, or at least dribbled from the holes in the pipes all day long. After my time at the brick factory, this was the first time I experienced the wonder of being able to drink whenever I became thirsty or whenever I had the urge. There was a crematorium in Buchenwald too, naturally, but only one, since that was not the camp's primary purpose, not its essence, its soul, its total meaning. I'd say that this was used only for those who passed away under natural conditions, one might say. In Buchenwald, so the news spread, presumably from the older prisoners, you needed to be very careful about the stone quarry, although, they added, it was not as much in use now as it had been when they first came here. The camp had been functioning for seven years, I was told, but there were those who came here from older camps, whose names I soon became familiar with, like Dachau, Oranienburg, and Sachsenhausen. Then I understood those somewhat forgiving, benign smiles on the faces of some of those well-dressed dignitaries on the other side of the wire fence, on whom I saw numbers in the five-, or even four- or three-digit categories.

Near our camp, I learned, there was a culturally important city, Weimar, whose fame I had already heard of at home. Here there had lived and worked, among others, that man whose poem "Wer reitet so spät durch Nacht und Wind?" [Who rides so late through night and the wind?] I knew by heart. His very hands, so went the story, here on the premises of the camp had planted a tree, which had now grown tall and shady and was complete with a commemorative inscription and was surrounded by a fence to protect it from us prisoners. Everything was taken into consideration here. I could easily understand those facial expressions back at Auschwitz. I have to say that I too very soon developed a liking for Buchenwald.

Zeitz, or rather the concentration camp named for this locality, was about a night's journey by freight train from Buchenwald and then a twenty- to twenty-five-minute march on foot, as one was accompanied by soldiers down a country road bordered by fields and well-cared-for farm landscapes— as I discovered for myself. This would be the final place of settlement—so they assured us—for those in our company whose names began with a letter preceding M in the alphabet. The others were bound for a labor camp in a city known to me for its historic fame, Magdeburg. We were informed of this in an enormously large plaza lighted by reflectors on the fourth evening in Buchenwald by prisoners wearing all kinds of insignia of dignity who had long lists in their hands. I only regretted that I was separated for good from many of the boys, especially Rozi, and that the accidental chance of the alphabet, which had determined our seats on the train, would unfortunately separate me from him forever.

I can say that there was nothing more wasteful, more exhausting, than those tedious rituals we had to pass through, it seemed, every time we arrived at a new concentration camp. After Auschwitz and Buchenwald, at least, this is what I expected at Zeitz, and what I once again experienced. Incidentally, I noticed right away this time that I had arrived at a smallish, poor, out-of-the-way, one might even say provincial concentration camp. Here I looked in vain for a bath or even a crematorium—apparently the prerequisites of only the more important camps. The area was once again an unvarying flatland, but from the end of the camp you could see some distant blue lines: the Thuringian Mountains, I was told by someone. The barbed-wire fence with four guard towers at the corners was adjacent to the highway. The camp itself was square—a large, dusty area, open on one side at the gate to the highway and surrounded on the other three sides by enormous canvas tents. The sole purpose, it turned out, of all that lengthy counting, mustering, pushing, and shoving was simply to assign every person in ten-man rows to his tent, or "block," as they called them.

I too wound up in one: to be quite precise, at the last right-hand tent of the last row as you were facing the gate with the tents behind you. I was assigned my block number according to the place in the row where I stood for a long time, until my legs fell asleep, under the merciless glare of the sun, which gradually became more and more unpleasant. I tried in vain to catch sight of the other boys: I was surrounded by total strangers. To my left a tall, thin, somewhat strange neighbor constantly mumbled to himself while he rocked his upper body rhythmically to and fro. To my right was a rather short, broad-shouldered man, who passed the time by spitting very precisely at regular intervals in front of him in the dust. He looked at me, first only cursorily, then in a more prolonged way, with lively, diagonally spaced, shiny buttonlike eyes. Under those eyes I saw a humorously small, almost boneless nose. He wore his convict's cap jauntily tilted to one side. "Well," he asked at the third glance, as I noticed that all his front teeth were missing, "well, where are you from?" When I answered, "From Budapest," he became very animated: Did the Ring still exist, and did the Number 6 tram still run, as it had when he left? I told him, "Yes, of course, it's all the same," and he seemed pleased. He was also curious to discover how and why I had ended up here, and I told him: "Very simply. They took me off the bus." "And?" he asked, after I finished. "No, that's it. Then they brought me here." He seemed somewhat surprised, like someone not completely aware of the circumstances at home, and I wanted to ask him . . . but I couldn't, because at that moment I got whacked in the face from the blind side.

Actually I was already sitting on the ground when I heard the noise and my left cheek began to burn. A man stood in front of me, dressed from top to toe in a black riding suit, wearing a black artist's cap. He had a beard and a narrow black mustache on his dark-skinned face, and I smelled—at least for me this was a surprising thing—the sweet smell of real perfume. From his confusing shouts I could only make out the repeated sound of *Ruhe*, that is, "silence." There was no question: he seemed to be a very high-ranking official, a fact underscored by his aristocratically low number as well as by the green triangle with the letter *Z* on one side of his chest and the silver whistle dangling on the other and, of course, by the white letters, *LA*, on his armband, which could be seen from afar. But still, I was very mad, because I was not yet used to being hit by anyone, and so, by my sitting and by my gestures I tried to give a strong vent to my anger. He must have noticed this, I think, because I saw that, even though he kept on shouting, the look of his dark, almost oily eyes gradually began to soften and then finally became an almost apologetic expression. During this time he studiously examined me from head to toe. Somehow I had an uncomfortable, tense feeling. Then he ran off into the middle of the separating crowd with the same stormy speed with which he had arrived.

When I raised myself up, my neighbor to the right soon asked me: "Did it hurt?" I told him in an intentionally loud voice: "No, not in the least." "Then," he added, "it might be a good idea if you wiped your nose." I touched it, and indeed, my finger was red. He showed me how to tilt my head back to stanch the bleeding, and he said about the dark man, "Gypsy." Then after some further deliberation, he added, "The guy's a fairy. No doubt about it." I didn't understand what he meant and asked him the meaning of the word. Then he laughed a little and said, "He's queer." Now I had a better idea; at least I think I did. "By the way," he remarked, extending his hand sideways, "I'm Bandi Citrom." In return I introduced myself too.

He had ended up here, I learned, from a labor camp. He had

been summoned right after they started the war because he was exactly twenty-one years old. He had qualified for labor service because of his age, blood, and state of health, and for four years he hadn't been home. He had just been in the Ukraine, defusing mines. "What about your teeth?" I asked. "They kicked them out," he answered. Then it was my turn to act surprised: "How come?" But he only called it a long story and spoke very little about it: he got along poorly with the group leader, and that's when, along with other things, the bone in his nose was broken. That's all I could pull out of him. The mine-field work he mentioned only briefly: "All you need is a shovel, a wire, and, of course, good luck," he said. That's why so few remained in the "penal squad" by the time the Germans arrived to replace the Hungarian boys, who were glad, because they were promised easier work and better circumstances. Then they too ended up at Auschwitz.

I was going to keep on quizzing him, but three men reappeared. Earlier, I had only caught one name from all that happened in front of me for ten minutes. To be more exact, I noticed the shouts of several voices calling the same name: "Dr. Kovacs!" In response, after some insistent calls, a modest-looking man, somewhat plump with a pudgy face, his head bald on the sides from the barber's razor and naturally bald in the center, stepped forward and pointed to two others. Then they all disappeared with the dark man, and only later, when the news finally reached me back there in the final rows, did I learn that we had just elected the block commander, or, as they called it, *Blockältester,* and then some *Stubendienst* (that is, as I loosely translated it for Bandi Citrom, who didn't know any German, "room-service men"). Now they wanted to teach us a few commands and the appropriate responses to them that they had been taught, and they told us that they would not teach us again. Some of these, such as "Achtung" [Attention], I was already familiar with, but not with others, such as "Korrigieret" (that is, "Adjust," referring to one's hat) and "Aus" [Out]. In response to these, they told us, we were to slap our hands against our thighs. All these we practiced repeatedly.

A Blockältester, we learned, had one more special job: he reported at the mustering, something he practiced several times in front of us, and one of the Stubendienst—a thick-set, scarlet-looking man with somewhat long, purple cheeks— stood in for the soldier. "Block 5," I heard him say, "is ready for inspection. Two hundred fifty inmates . . . there . . . etcetera, etcetera, present," and from this I surmised that, since I was a tenant of the fifth block, it contained 250 men. After a few rehearsals, all this was clear, understandable, and perfectly functional. Everyone thought so.

Then some idle moments followed, and when I noticed some sort of a mound with a long bar above it next to our tent, I asked Bandi Citrom what he thought it could be. "Water closets," he declared without a moment's hesitation. He shook his head a little when he saw that I wasn't familiar with the expression. "It's obvious that you've been sitting on your mama's skirt all this time," he said. Then he explained himself with a short declarative sentence and added, to quote him in full: "Well, by the time we shit them full, we'll be free." I laughed, but he remained as serious as someone who is genuinely convinced (or, I'd say, determined) that this was the case. But he couldn't elaborate on this idea, because right then three earnest-looking and well-groomed soldiers appeared from the direction of the gate, approaching without hurrying. They seemed obviously at home and very confident of themselves. In response to them, the Blockältester called out, now with a new, somehow eager, and showy color in his voice: "Achtung! Mützen . . . ab!" [Attention! Caps . . . off!]. Then, as did everyone else, including myself, he yanked off his cap.

8

Only in Zeitz did I realize that captivity also has its gray, everyday days, or, rather, that true captivity is really a row of gray, everyday days. It seemed as if I had been in a similar situation once before, when we were headed for Auschwitz. There too everything had depended on time and on everyone's own capability. But in Zeitz—to continue the metaphor—I had to admit that the train had stopped. Seen from another angle, however—and this is equally true—the train went on with such speed that I couldn't keep track of the many changes before me, around me, and even within myself. One thing I can say: as far as I was concerned, I honestly tried out every pitfall that may have arisen during the journey.

In any case, we begin something new with the best of intentions—even in a concentration camp. At least that was my experience. For starters I had become a pretty good prisoner; the future would take care of the rest. At least that was my attitude. I based my whole conduct on this idea, just the same way, incidentally, as I observed that others were doing. I soon noticed that those favorable opinions that I had been given in Auschwitz concerning labor camps as institutions were probably based on somewhat exaggerated information. I didn't, and after all I couldn't, however, directly perceive the extent of these exaggerations, or, even more important, their many consequences in full. This was the same with the others, I can say with certainty. I observed them and sensed the same lack of comprehension in the approximately two thousand prisoners in our camp—except, of course, in the suicides. But their cases were quite rare, in no way normal, and in no case exemplary, as everyone admitted. The news of such events only occasionally reached my ears. I heard how friends discussed and debated—some with open disapproval, others more sympathetically—their dead acquaintances with pity, in such a way that one attempted to form a judgment regarding this very rare, far removed, somehow almost inexplicable, perhaps somewhat irresponsible, perhaps a little admirable, but at any rate over-quick action.

What was important was that you should not let yourself go: somehow things would work out, because it never happened that they didn't work out. So Bandi Citrom taught me as he, in turn, had been taught this wisdom earlier in his labor camp. The first and most important detail was to keep well washed (parallel rows of troughs together with iron pipes complete with holes stood in the fresh air on the side of the camp facing the highway). Equally essential was the careful use of one's daily portion of food—whether one had it or not. From the bread, for example, regardless of the self-discipline that this rule required, one had to save a piece for morning coffee and also a piece for lunch—with the constant control of our thoughts from wandering toward our pockets, but mostly the control of our hands. Only in this way could we avoid the excruciating thought: "We have no food." I learned a lot: what I believed to be handkerchiefs were foot cloths; at the evening mustering, or while marching, the only place of safety was in the middle of the line; at soup distribution time, we should try to avoid being in front and should stay in the rear, where presumably they would serve us from the bottom of the pot and consequently from the thick of the soup; we could hammer one side of our soup spoon into a functional knife. All this useful knowledge and a lot else I learned or observed from Bandi Citrom, and I tried eagerly to apply these rules.

I would never have believed this one simple fact: nowhere is a kind of ordered life-style, a kind of exemplary behavior, even an ethic, as important as in captivity, it seems. It was enough to give one a moment's reflection in the proximity of Block 1, where the oldest inhabitants lived. On their chests the yellow triangle explained everything important, and the letter *L* told us the incidental information that they were from distant Latvia, or more precisely from the city of Riga, as I found out. Among them, you might find those strange creatures who had quizzed me at length at first. Looked at from a detached point of view, they were a bunch of ancient old men, with their heads buried in their shoulders, with their noses protruding from their faces, and with their filthy convicts' clothes hanging loosely from their hunched-up shoulders. They reminded me of those winter blackbirds, eternally cold, freezing, even on the hottest summer's day. It was as if they were asking with every stiff, halting step: Is such exertion, indeed, worth the effort? These moving question marks—for, not only on account of their appearance but also on account of their behavior, I can characterize them in no other way—were known in the concentration camp by the name of Muslims, as I was told. Bandi Citrom immediately warned me about them: "When one looks at them, one loses all desire to live," he said, and there was some truth to his statement, even if I found out later that much more than that is required for one to lose the desire to live.

Above all, there was the tool of stubbornness. Although some things might have been missing at Zeitz, this quality was not among them, and at times, I noticed, it could be of tremendous benefit to us. For instance, I learned more from Bandi Citrom about that queer company, fraternity, race, or whatever you may call them of whom one example, standing on my immediate left in the row as we arrived, already surprised me a lot. Bandi Citrom told me that we called them Finns. And really, when you asked them where they lived, they answered—that is, if they thought you were worthy of an answer—for example, "Fin Minkacs." Bandi Citrom knew their fraternity already from his labor camp, and he thought little of them. They were everywhere—at work, at mustering, at marches, mumbling their prayers endlessly like a debt that can never be-paid off and rocking rhythmically back and forth. If, during this time, they pulled their lips to the side in order to whisper, "A knife is for sale," we paid no attention to them. And we listened even less, regardless of the temptation, especially in the mornings, when they whispered, "Soup is for sale." As strange as it sounds, they didn't live on soup, and not even on the occasional sausage; they ate nothing that was not in strict accordance with their religion. "But what do they live on, then?" someone would ask, and Bandi Citrom would reply: "You shouldn't worry about them." And yes indeed, obviously, they did survive. Among themselves and with the Latvians they spoke Yiddish, but they also knew German, Slovak, and God knows what else, with the exception of Hungarian—unless, of course, they were talking business.

Once it happened—and I couldn't avoid it—I wound up in their headquarters. "Reds di jiddis?" [Do you speak Yiddish?] was their first question. When I told them no, unfortunately not, they were finished with me; they treated me as if I were a nonentity. I tried to speak up, to make them take note of me, but it was fruitless. "You are no Jew." They shook their heads, and I was entirely perplexed to see people who, after all, were supposed to be so experienced in business affairs insist so irrationally on a thing that was much more of a loss and a disadvantage to them than a profit, when you considered the end results. Then, that day I also experienced that very same tenseness, that same itchy feeling and clumsiness that came over me when I was with them, that I had occasionally felt at home: as if I weren't entirely okay, as if I didn't entirely conform to the ideal; in other words, somehow as if I were Jewish. That was a rather strange feeling, because, after all, I was among Jews and in a concentration camp.

At other times I was a little astonished about Bandi Citrom. Both at work and at rest I often heard him sing his favorite song, and so I learned it from him quickly. It was a song for the penal service that he had brought from the labor camp:

In the Ukraine we pick mines
But even there we won't be cowards.

That is how it started, and I particularly came to appreciate the last stanza:

And if a good friend, a good pal, dies
Then in spite of all that waits for us,
Our sweet, dear homeland,
We shall never, never be untrue to you.

It was beautiful. That was undeniable. Its melody was a little sad, rather slow, not at all perky, and of course, the words of the poem didn't lose their effect on me either. It was only that they somehow reminded me of the military policeman, the one on the train some time ago who had reminded us of our Hungarianness. After all, they were also punished by our homeland, strictly speaking. I once mentioned this to Bandi. He found no argument to counter my observation, but he seemed a little confused, I'd say almost annoyed. The next day, at one time or another, he started to whistle, hum, and then sing that song, all lost in thought, as if everything was forgotten. His other often-repeated thought was "I shall again walk the cobblestones of Nefelejcs Street," that is, where he had lived, and he mentioned this street and his house number so frequently and emotionally that finally I also became familiar with its attraction, almost as if I too were longing to be there, even though in my own memory it was a small, insignificant side street somewhere in the neighborhood of the Keleti train station.

Quite frequently Bandi talked about and reminded me of certain places, squares, streets, and houses, of the signs and the shop windows with their well-known slogans and ads—in other words, as he put it, "of the lights of Pest." I couldn't help but correct him on this account, explaining that these lights no longer existed because of the new regulations concerning the darkening of windows and that, in fact, the bombs had changed the city landscape here and there. He listened to me, but the information wasn't to his liking. The next day at the first opportunity, he again started in on the lights.

But who could be aware of all the variations of stubbornness? I have to say that I could have chosen from many different styles in Zeitz, had I been able to. I heard a lot said about the past and the future and a very great deal about freedom here among the prisoners, more than I had ever heard anywhere else. This was quite naturally understandable, I think. Others, again, found some particular joy in aphorisms, jokes, and teasing. I also heard these, of course.

There was an hour in the day, between our return from the factory and mustering—an important, always-active hour, full of relief, which I for one liked best and anticipated eagerly. Incidentally this was also the dinner hour. I was pressing through the crowds in the courtyard, where people were buzzing, making business deals, or chitchatting, when someone bumped into me. From under the wide convict's cap, tiny worried eyes sitting over a typical nose in a typical face looked at me. "Look at you!" we both said, almost together, as he recognized me and I him: it was the man with the bad luck. His immediate reaction was to be overjoyed, and he wanted to know where I was staying. I told him Block 5. "Too bad," he said, because he lived somewhere else. He complained of "never seeing his acquaintances," and when I let him know that I didn't either, he turned quite sad. "We lost sight of each other. We all lost sight of each other," he observed, shaking his head with some veiled meaning in his words that I failed to comprehend. But then, suddenly, his face lighted up again. "Do you know," he asked, pointing toward his chest, "what the letter *U* means here?" I told him that of course I knew. It meant *Ungar,* that is, "Hungarian." "No," he answered, "it means *unschuldig*" (that is, "innocent"). Then he laughed a little and nodded for a long time with a thoughtful face, like someone who enjoys his idea. I'm uncertain why. And I spotted the same reaction in others too, who told me the same joke quite often at the beginning of my stay in the camp. It was as if they were drawing some kind of reassuring, warming, strength-giving feeling from it. At least that was the implication given by that always-identical laugh, that same softening of the face, that painful and yet somehow admiring expression in the smile with which they invariably told the joke or listened to it, somewhat the way one hears a heart-rending piece of music or a very moving story.

But still, in all the people I noticed the same eagerness, the same good intentions. They too were determined to prove themselves to be model prisoners. No question about it: That was in our own self-interest. That was what was required by the circumstances. That is what life, so to speak, demanded. For instance, when the order of the rows was perfectly correct and the numbers were right, mustering took less time—at least initially. When we were diligent at work, we avoided beatings—at least most of the time. Yet still, at least at the beginning, we were not entirely motivated by this profit; our thoughts could not have been entirely directed by this hope for gain, I have to say in all honesty.

There was, for example, work, which started the first afternoon. Our chief job was the unloading of a wagon of gray gravel. So when Bandi Citrom said—after receiving the permission of the guard (a lively, but at first glance rather sheepish-looking soldier) as we stripped our upper bodies—"Come on, let's show them what Budapest people can do!" he meant it very seriously. (Incidentally, that was when I first saw his yellowish-brown skin with his large smooth muscles flexing, and a dark birthmark under his chest on the left.) And I must say that, considering, after all, that I had a pitchfork in my hand for the very first time in my life, both our guards and another man who looked like a foreman, probably from the factory, seemed quite pleased. This, in turn, only increased our speed and efforts, of course. When, however, after a while a burning sensation announced itself in my palms (my hands really started burning) and I noticed that from the tips of my fingers my palms were all bloody and our guard then asked, "What's the matter?" I laughed and showed him my hands. He responded by suddenly becoming very serious and pulling on his gun belt. He said: "Arbeiten! Aber los!" [Work! Get going!]. Then, finally, it was only natural that my interest changed.

From that point on I watched for only one thing: when his

eyes were not resting on me, then I could steal a tiny rest or load as little as possible on the shovel, pitchfork, or spade. I have to say that I made excellent progress in perfecting these little evasions, and I acquired greater facility, experience, and knowledge at this than in the process of any other work that I performed. But after all, who profits from this? As I remember, the "expert" once asked this. I must insist: something was wrong here, some barrier, some mistake, some failure. The least sign of praise, a single word, a tiny ray of hope here or there, no more than a spark, would have done me a great deal more good. Because on the personal level, really, what do we hold against one another? And even in captivity, a sense of pride and vanity still remained with us. Who, after all, does not require a little kindness in secret? And one can achieve a great deal more with some kind words, I always thought.

But such experiences could not really shake me. A train too was still running, and if I looked ahead, I sensed a destination somewhere in the far distance. During this first period of time—the Golden Age, as Bandi Citrom and I came to call it later—Zeitz proved to be quite a bearable place, provided that you behaved well and had a bit of luck—that is, for the time being, until the future liberated you, of course. Every week we had one-half of a regular portion of bread twice, one-third three times, and one-fourth only twice; supplements were quite frequent. Once a week we had boiled potatoes (six of them were served in our caps, but with this, obviously, we could get no supplement). Once a week we had porridge. The dewy summer dawn, a clear sky, and of course the steaming coffee quickly made you forget the first annoyance of early waking (on these occasions you had to be fast at the latrines because very soon calls for a mustering echoed about). The morning mustering was, of necessity, short, because, after all, work awaited us, urged us on.

One of the factory's side gates that we prisoners could use lay to the left of the highway against a sandy hill, approximately a ten-to-fifteen-minute walk from the camp. From a distance you could hear the buzzing, clinking, purring, breathing, the three or four cranky coughs of the iron throats. The factory was greeting you. With its main and side streets, its cranes, its earth-eating machines, and the labyrinth of its chimneys, rails, cooling towers, and a net of pipes and shop buildings, it was a genuine city unto itself. The many ditches, holes, ruins, and torn lines and cables attested to visits by airplanes. Its name, as I had already discovered during the first lunch break, was Brabay, which stands for Braun-Kohl-Benzin Aktiengesell-schaft, an abbreviation once used on the stock market, I was told by a corpulent man who was leaning on his elbows, huff-ing tiredly, and fishing out some chewed-up piece of bread from his pocket. They said in the camp—always with some humor—that he had once also owned some of the shares in this enterprise, although I never heard this directly from him. I heard that here they also worked on oil production—and the smell immediately reminded me of the Csepel oil refinery—but with an invention that enabled them to refine not from crude oil, but from coal. I found the idea interesting, but that was not what was expected of me, naturally; I could see that.

The assignments by the "work commandant" were always exciting events. Some prisoners swore by the shovel, others by the pickax. Some argued the advantage of hanging cables, oth-ers again preferred handling the mortar-mixing machine, and who knows what hidden reason, what suspicious predilection, drew some to the sewage work, with yellow mud or black oil up to their waists. No one doubted the existence of some reason, though, since the Latvians and their friends, the Finns, often followed this persuasion. Only once a day did the word *retreat* have a high-trilled, sweetly sad, expanding, long, and inviting melody—namely in the evening, when it signaled the time for our homeward journey.

In the foofaraw around the washbasins, Bandi Citrom pres-sured for some room with a shout: "Make some room, Mus-lims." Not a spot on my body escaped his inspection: "Clean your genital area too. That's where the lice live," he com-manded, and I obeyed him laughingly. This was when that special hour began, the time when this, that, and the other thing was to be done. This was the time for jokes and complaints, visits, conferences, business transactions, the exchange of information, as well as the familiar clatter of pots that could only be interrupted by the announcement mobilizing everyone and inspiring everyone to a quick response: "Mustering time!" How long that lasted was a question of luck. But after one, two, or at the very longest three hours (during which the reflectors also were turned on), there was a great rush down the narrow path of the tent, bordered on both sides by three long rows of boxes, our places of rest.

Then for a while the tent was a place of dimness and whispers. This was the hour for stories of the past, of the future, of freedom. I found out that at home everybody was perfectly happy and mostly rich. At such times I also learned what people usually had for dinner. Furthermore, I heard some talk of certain "man-to-man" subjects. Then they also mentioned—something I never heard of later—that according to some people's suspicions, our soup was laced with a calming chemical, namely bromium, for a certain reason. At least that's what some of the men said with a mysterious expression on their faces and in complete agreement among themselves.

On these occasions without fail Bandi Citrom also mentioned Nefelejcs Street, the lights, and—especially in the beginning, even though I had no comments on the subject—the "Budapest women." At other times some suspicious mumbling effectively halted a song, and in the muffled candlelight I noticed something in one of the corners of the tent. I heard it was Friday evening and that a priest was there, a rabbi. I stumbled over there, on top of the boxes, in order to see for myself, and indeed, there in the middle of a group of people was the rabbi I knew. He practiced his piety in his convict's garb and cap, but I paid little attention to him because I far preferred sleeping to praying.

Bandi Citrom and I lived on the top floor. We shared our box with two other sleepers. Both were young, affable, and also from Budapest. Under us was wood, with straw placed on it, and on top of that was a canvas sheet. Two of us owned a blanket together, but during summer even that was too much. Our box was not exactly spacious. If I turned, my neighbor had to turn too; if my neighbor pulled up his legs, I had to pull mine up too. But still, sleep is deep and all-erasing. Those were the golden days indeed.

9

I started to notice some changes a little later, mostly concerning the food portions. I—we—could only guess why the days of the one-half bread portions disappeared so quickly. In their place came the period of a third and then a fourth, and the supplements were no longer assured either. That's when the train of events began to slow down, and finally they came to a halt. I tried to look ahead, but my vision only extended to tomorrow, and tomorrow was the same day as this one—that is, if we were lucky. My spirits faltered, my energy declined. Every day getting up was a little more difficult, and every day I lay down to rest a little more tired. I was a little more hungry. I lived a little more forcedly. Somehow everything began to be more difficult. I even became a burden to myself. I no longer was—or should I say, we weren't good prisoners all the time, and the effect of this we could soon observe on the soldiers, and of course chiefly on our representatives—first of all on the *Lagerältester* [camp commander], because of his rank.

He could still be seen anywhere and at any time dressed entirely in black. From the whistle that signaled wake-up in the morning to the evening, he examined everything, and there was a lot of talk about his quarters up there somewhere in front. His language was German, his blood gypsy. We only knew him by the nickname Gypsy. This was the chief reason why they had assigned him to the concentration camp. The second was his deviant quality that Bandi Citrom had pinpointed at first glance. The green color of his triangle, on the other hand, warned everyone that he had killed and robbed a supposedly older and—so they said—very wealthy lady from whom he had received his support. And so, for the first time in my life, I was actually able to set eyes on a genuine robber-murderer.

His job was the enforcement of the law. His work was to keep order and justice in our camp. At first glance, this was not particularly encouraging, we all believed, myself included. On the other hand, though, I had to admit that under certain circumstances such things become confusing. I for one had a lot more trouble with one of the Stubendienst, for instance, even though he was an unquestionably honorable man. That's why his acquaintances had elected him, along with the block commander, Dr. Kovacs (whose title, incidentally, did not denote a medical doctor, but a lawyer, as I was told). Both men came from the same place, a lovely region of the Balaton called Siófok. Kovacs was a ruddy-faced man whose first name everyone knew: Fodor.

Now whether or not it was true, the general opinion was that the gypsy Lagerältester enjoyed using his stick or his fist at will because, according at least to gossip, this supposedly gave him some pleasure in his dealings with men, with boys, and occasionally even with women—or so the well informed told us. In these cases, however, keeping order is no pretense but a "genuine requirement" with a general benefit, and he never forgot to mention this, of course. On the other hand, keeping order was never complete and now was increasingly less so. And so he was forced to use the long iron handle of the soup spoon to hit those who were pushing near the pot. This was the way we might be treated if we didn't follow the rules of how to approach the pot and place our plates against a predetermined spot on its rim. Among the victims were those whose hands sent pots of soup flying through the air, because these culprits had jeopardized his work and the place of us who stood behind in the line voicing our approval. He also dragged late sleepers by their feet out of their boxes because the sin of one created problems for the innocent as well. There was a difference, I could see, in the people's intention, naturally, but as I said, at a certain point such distinctions disappear and the results become identical, regardless of how you look at them.

Aside from him, there was also a German Kapo there with a yellow armband and impeccably ironed, striped clothes. Fortunately I didn't see much of him, but then later, much to my surprise, some black armbands with a more modest *Vorarbeiter* inscription began to show up on the sleeves of some of us. I was around when a man from our block—until then a not particularly noteworthy and, if my memory serves me correctly, a not very highly esteemed or well-known person who, however, was strong and well-built—first appeared at dinner with a brand new ribbon on his sleeve. Now, I saw, he was no longer that same unknown man; from all directions friends and acquaintances pushed to get near him. He was surrounded by congratulations, good wishes, and expressions of delight at his promotion, as hands were extended everywhere. Some were shaken; others were not. I noticed that those whose hands he ignored quickly disappeared from the scene. And later followed the—to me at least—very solemn moment when, amid great attentiveness and some sort of respectful or almost inspired silence, with great dignity, not in the least hurriedly and not at all quickly, in the cross fire of admiring or envious eyes, he stepped forward to receive his second serving, which was now his due according to his rank, and that came from the very bottom of the pot and was served by a Stubendienst with the respect owed to equals.

At another time the letters glared at me from the arm of a trim, barrel-chested man with a firm step. I recognized him immediately: he was an officer from Auschwitz. One day I ended up working under him, and I can say that it's true that he went through fire for his good men, but he extended no laurels to those who let others do their work, those who were lazybones—as he himself put it at the beginning of the working day. So the next day Bandi Citrom and I sneaked over to another commander.

I was struck by one other change, and that, interestingly enough, occurred mostly in outsiders, such as the factory people, our guards, and even some of the officials of our camp. What I noticed was that they became transformed. At first I couldn't explain this alteration: somehow they all appeared beautiful, at least in my eyes. Only later did I realize that all signs indicated that maybe we were the ones who had changed, of course, but this was more difficult to perceive. When, for example, I looked at Bandi Citrom, I noticed nothing special about him. But I tried to remember my first impression of him standing to my right in the row or at work. I had been struck by his almost textbook-illustrating physique, his expanding and contracting muscles in constant movement, and then when I compared that impression with my view of him now, I had to be a little puzzled. Only then did I understand that time can deceive our eyes.

Here is how a perfectly observable string of events could have escaped my attention, events affecting a whole family, the Kollmanns, for example. Everybody knew them at the camp. They came from a place called Kisvárda, which had several other inhabitants here, and from these people's remarks I concluded that at home the Kollmanns must have been highly respected. There were three of them: a small bold father, an older son, and a younger son. The sons had faces almost identical to each other's but very different from their father's—similar, I guess, to their mother's—with the same blond manes and the same blue eyes. Whenever possible, the three were together, hand in hand. After a while I noticed that the father kept dropping behind and that the two boys had to assist him, pulling him along by the hand. Somewhat later the father was no longer beside them. Soon after that the older boy needed to pull the younger one along the same way. Still later the younger one disappeared, and then the older boy was left to drag himself along, and then I didn't see him anymore either. All of this, as I said, I noticed, but not in the same way as later, when I started to fit the pieces together and could sum up and recall the events step by step. I had become used to every new step gradually, and this hadn't given me the detachment I needed to actually notice what was happening.

Yet I had also changed, it seems, because Leather-Worker, whom I saw exiting with great familiarity from one of the corners of the kitchen tent—I learned that he had found himself an enviable position among those great dignitaries, the potato-peelers—didn't want to recognize me at all. I assured him that it was "me, from Shell," and asked him if by any chance some leftovers could be found in the kitchen, some remnants, maybe, from the bottoms of the pots. He said he'd check, and he wondered if I had any cigarettes on me because the kitchen foreman was "dying for cigarettes," as he put it. I said that I had none, and then he left. After waiting for a while, I realized that waiting any longer would be a total waste of time and that friendship, also, is a finite thing, whose boundaries are defined by the laws of life.

On another occasion it was I who failed to recognize a strange creature: he was stumbling along in the direction of the latrines. His convict's cap slid down to his ears. His face was a map of caves, hills, and valleys. His nose was yellow, and at its tip was a shiny, trembling drop of water. "Silky Boy," I called to him. He didn't even look up. He just kept on shuffling while holding his pants up with one hand. I thought to myself: "Well, I would never have believed it." At another time I think I noticed Smoker, only he was even more yellow and more skinny, and his eyes were larger and more feverish. This was the time when in the block commander's reports in the morning and at the evening mustering certain calls became a permanent fixture, varying only in numbers: "Two to sick bay," or "Five to sick bay," or "Thirteen to sick bay," and so on. And then an entirely new concept arose: the diminishing, the disappearance of certain people that was referred to as an *Abgang*. No, under certain circumstances the best of intentions is not sufficient. While I was still at home, I had read that with time and at the cost of a certain effort, one can grow accustomed even to prison life. This is probably so. I have no doubt, let's say, that one can feel at home in a regular, respectable (how shall I say it?) civil prison, for example. Only in a concentration camp, from my experience, there is no possibility of this. And I can say with assurance that, at least as far as I am concerned, this was not for the lack of trying or for the lack of good intentions. The problem was, simply, that they didn't give you enough time to try.

I know of three means of escape from a concentration camp, because I either saw, heard, or experienced them. I lived by the first one, the most modest, perhaps: there is one aspect of human nature that, I had learned in school, is also a person's inalienable right. It is true that our imagination remains free even in captivity. I could, for instance, achieve this freedom while my hands were busy with a shovel or a pickax—with a moderate exertion, limiting myself to the most essential movements only. I myself was simply not there. But still, imagination is only free within certain boundaries, as I had experienced. For I could have, after all, wished myself anywhere—Calcutta, Florida, the most beautiful spots of the world. But still, these fantasies were not sufficiently tenable. I couldn't, so to speak, give them credibility, and so I usually found myself back home. Without any doubt, I was no less adventurous doing this than I would have been, let's say, by putting myself in Calcutta. Only here I experienced a certain modesty (I could almost say a certain exertion that balanced and at the same time validated my efforts).

For instance, I very soon realized that I had not lived correctly. I had not made good use of my days at home. I had much too much to regret. For example, I remembered that there were foods that I had been finicky about. I had fiddled with them and then pushed them aside, for the very simple reason that I hadn't liked them. At that moment I found such finickiness impossible to comprehend and an irreparable loss. There was also that senseless arguing back and forth between my father and my mother on my account. "When I return home," I thought (and I thought this in a simple, self-explanatory way like one who is interested in nothing but questions following a perfectly natural turn of events), "when I return, then I shall put an end to all this." There had to be peace, I decided.

There was a lot at home that had made me nervous, then even—regardless of how ridiculous it seemed—had made me afraid. For instance, I was afraid of certain subjects in my studies, of the professors, of being called upon and maybe failing in my answers, and finally of my father, when I had to report my progress. Now over and over again I recalled these fears only with amusement, so that I could now imagine and relive them and smile.

But in my favorite pastime I invariably imagined a whole day at home, from morning until night when possible, constantly normal and average. Imagining a special, a particularly perfect day took the same energy. I very seldom chose to imagine a bad day with an early rising, school worries, a bad lunch, and a lot of opportunities missed, lost, or not even noticed. I was now setting everything straight with the greatest perfection while here in the camp, I have to say. I have heard it said before, and now I can attest to its truth: narrow prison walls cannot set limits to the flights of our imagination. Only one problem existed: when my fantasies carried me to such distant lands that I forgot to use my hands, soon the reality of the real place asserted itself with the most pressing and determined demands.

At about this time a new phenomenon arose at morning mustering when the numbers present didn't jibe—as happened at this time in Block 4 just next to us. Everybody knew full well what could result when a wake-up call in a concentration camp failed to wake up those who no longer wanted to be wakened. And there were those. This was the second route of escape. Who was not tempted—once, at least once—to do this? Who remained completely untouched, especially in the morning when we woke up for another fresh day in an already noisy tent surrounded by neighbors who were already preparing themselves? I would definitely have tried it, if it had not been for Bandi Citrom's strongly preventing me. After all, coffee is not all that important, and we could get up in time for the muster. I felt certain of that. We couldn't, of course, stay in our sleeping places, since, after all, no one could be that childish. We would have to get up, normally and honestly like the others, and then we would find a hiding place, an entirely safe little cranny. I would bet a hundred against one. Just yesterday, or perhaps even earlier, we spotted a place, looked it over; it struck our eyes by chance, without any plans or intentions, as a possibility for ourselves. Now we remember it. We crawl, for instance, under the lowest box. Or we seek out this unique 100-percent-safe cranny, nook, corner, or indentation. There, then, we cover ourselves completely with straw and blankets. All this time we keep thinking that we shall attend the muster ourselves. I tell you, there were times when I understood this feeling well, very well indeed.

The more courageous ones among us could even possibly think, "Well, one person might slide by unnoticed." They could miscount, for example. After all, we are all only human, so *one* missing person today, just this morning, is not going to stand out, and by evening we could make certain that the numbers will jibe. The even more daring could think that in that secure spot they wouldn't be found by anyone, not in any way. But the truly determined ones weren't even considering this, because they were convinced—and there were times when I too felt this way—that an hour's worth of good sleep is worth any price, any risk.

But they rarely if ever steal that much sleep, because everything moves swiftly in the morning. In a jiffy a search group is formed, led by the Lagerältester, dressed in black, with his freshly shaven, stiff mustache and his perfume, while close behind him go the two German Kapos, followed by the Block-ältester and the Stubendienst with sticks and clubs all ready in hand. They head straight for Block 4. From inside there is noise, chaos, and a few moments later—lo and behold!—the triumphant shouts of victorious detectives. Some whining, mixed with the shouts, becomes progressively thinner, then silent, and soon the hunters reappear. What they drag from the tent—a motionless, dead mass, a messy bundle of rags—they toss to the outer side of the row. I try not to look. Still one and another broken part, one or another still recognizable detail or memorable characteristic draws my glance, and I realize whom this has been about: the man with bad luck. Then: "Arbeits-kommandos antreten!" [Work commanders begin!]. We can now expect that, today, the soldiers will be more severe.

Finally there is the third, the most literal meaning of escape to consider. It seems there had been one example of that, only once, in our camp. There were three real escapees, all three Latvians, who were experienced and versed in the geography of the area and the German language, secure in what they were doing—so the rumor went. I must say that, after the initial reactions of respect and our secret gloating over our guards and, yes, here and there even admiration and an impulse to consider following their example after weighing the pros and cons of the event, we all became rather angry at them during the night around two or three o'clock when, as punishment for their deed, we were still forced to stand, or rather stagger, at a mustering. The next evening on their return I tried not to look to the right. For there stood three chairs, and on them were three men, or rather three manlike creatures. I found it easier not to ask who they were or what was written in large primitive letters on the paper tablets dangling from their necks. Still, the information reached me, because it was long remembered and recalled in the camp. It read: "Hurrah! Ich bin wieder da!" that is, "Hurrah, I am back!"

I also saw some kind of a construction, something a little reminiscent of the rug-beating racks in yards at home, with three looped ropes hanging down from them, and I under-stood that this was a gallows. Naturally there was no mention of dinner, but rather an immediate call to muster, and then "Das ganze Lager: Achtung!" [The whole camp: Attention!] was commanded by the Lagerältester himself at the top of his voice up there in front. The usual group of punishment-executors gathered, and after some further waiting, the rep-resentatives of the military officials also appeared, and then everything took its course (how shall I say?) according to rules and order—fortunately far away from us, up front, close to the bathing facilities. I didn't look in that direction.

Instead, I looked to the left, where suddenly a voice arose, some mumbling, some sort of a melody. There in a row I saw a thin, extended neck and a shaky head, but mostly a nose and a gigantic wet eye that at this moment seemed bathed in some unreal light: it was the rabbi. Soon I understood his words as well, all the more so since gradually several people in his row took up the song. The Finns, for example, all did, and many others did as well. And I don't know how, but it spread. It invaded other blocks too, as I noticed more and more moving lips and careful, cautious, yet determinedly rocking shoulders, necks, and heads. All the while the murmurings here in the middle of the row were barely audible but constant, like some rumbling from beneath the earth: "Jiskadal, vöjiskadal," was intoned repeatedly, and even I knew that this was the so-called Kaddish, the prayer of Jews to honor their dead. Possibly this, too, was just simply an aspect of stubbornness, a final and perhaps—I had to admit—somewhat forced one because it was pretailored, predesigned, and useless (because, after all, nothing had changed up front, and except for the few, final struggles of the ones hanging, nothing had moved, nothing was affected by these words). Yet I somehow understood the emotion with which the rabbi's face seemed to dissolve and the force by which even his nostrils trembled in such a strange way. It was as if that long-awaited moment had arrived, that certain victorious moment of whose advent, I recalled, he had already spoken back in the brick factory. And indeed, at that moment and for the first time (I can't explain why), I too felt a sense of loss, even a little envy. This was the first time I regretted a little that I wasn't able—if only for a few phrases—to pray in the language of the Jews.

But no stubbornness, prayer, or any form of escape could free us from one thing: hunger. Of course even at home I had experienced—or at least I had thought I was experiencing—hunger. I had been hungry in the brick factory, on the train, in

Auschwitz, and even in Buchenwald, but I had never experienced the sensation this way for such a long time—a long distance, one might say. I had become a pit, a form of empty space, and my every effort, every attempt, was directed toward eliminating, stuffing, or quieting this bottomless pit, this constantly voracious void. I had eyes only for this: my mind could be in the service only of this, my every action was motivated only by this, and if I didn't eat wood, iron, or stones, it was only for the simple reason that they were not chewable or digestible. For instance, I did try to eat sand, and if I spotted some grass, I didn't hesitate for a moment. Unfortunately grass was difficult to find both in the factory and in the camp.

For a solitary tiny pointed onion they were asking two slices of bread, and for the same price those lucky owners sold sugar beets and turnips. I usually preferred the latter because they were juicier and almost always larger, even though the experts considered sugar beets to be richer in nutrition and calories. But who could be choosy, even if I myself took no great pleasure in their tough texture and sharp taste? They satisfied me, though, and I also received some consolation from observing others while they were eating. Lunch was brought to the factory for our guards, and I never took my eyes away from them. I have to say, however, that this gave me very little pleasure. They gobbled everything up quickly and didn't even chew; they rushed through the whole meal. I could see that they were ignorant of what they were doing.

At other times I was assigned to the workshop. Here master craftsmen opened up the lunches they had brought from home, and I remember I watched a huge yellow hand, full of bumps, for an interminably long time as it kept lifting long green beans out of a tall jar, one after the other. I watched, I admit, with a vague, uncertain hope. But this bumpy hand—I got to know its every bump, its every predictable move—continued to go back and forth between the jar and the mouth, in an uninterrupted commerce. After a while even that view was hidden by the man's back as he finally turned away—out of humaneness, I understood—though I wanted to say to him, "Please go on, continue, because as far as I'm concerned, I value just the sight, since even this is better than nothing."

For the first time I bought the previous day's potato peelings—a complete potful—from a Finn. He had carried it out during the midday break, slowly, comfortably, and luckily, on the day when Bandi Citrom wasn't my boss, so he couldn't object. The Finn placed it in front of himself, took a torn piece of paper and rock salt from it—all this slowly, without any haste—and tasted a tiny portion before, almost as an aside, he called over: "For sale!" Usually the price is two slices of bread or the margarine; he asked for one-half of my evening soup. I tried to bicker with him, invoking everything, even our equality. "You're not a Jew," he said. He shook his head the way the Finns usually do. I asked him: "Then why on earth am I here?" "How should I know?" he answered, shrugging his shoulders. I said to him: "Rotten Jew!" "You still can't have it for less," he answered. I concluded by buying it anyway for the price he was asking, and I can't figure out how he managed to show up at night at just the second they were measuring out my soup, but he did, and I also don't know how he ferreted out the information that we were going to have milksop for dinner.

I can declare that there are certain ideas that one can only fully comprehend in a concentration camp. For instance, the favorite hero of my silly childhood fairy tales was "the poor boy" or "the wandering boy" who, in order to gain the hand of a princess in marriage, agreed to serve a king because the price was only seven days of work. "But seven days are seven years," said the king to him, and I can well say the same about the concentration camp. I would have never believed, for instance, that I could be transformed into a dried-up old man so quickly. At home this process takes time—fifty or sixty years at least. Here three months sufficed for my body to desert me. I can say for certain that nothing is more awkward, nothing more discouraging, than noticing day after day, keeping track day after day, of how much we have rotted away. At home, even though I paid little attention, I was still generally in harmony with my body. I was fond of, let us call it, this machine.

I recall a summer afternoon as I was reading an exciting novel in a cool room, while my hand stroked the golden-haired, obedient soft skin of my muscular, sunburnt thighs with pleasant absentmindedness. Now that same skin hung in loose folds: it was yellow and desiccated, covered by all kinds of growths, brown circles, cuts, bumps, and scales that, especially between my fingers, kept itching unpleasantly. "Fungus," Bandi Citrom declared with an expert nod when I showed them to him. I was simply open-mouthed at the speed, at the limitless quickness, with which every day the elasticity of the cover of my bones, my flesh, diminished, atrophied, melted, or disappeared. Every day I was surprised by some new happening, some new flaw, some new atrocity on this progressively strange and progressively alien object that once had been my good friend: my body. I could no longer glance at my body without some feeling of disgust or alienation. After a while I no longer undressed to wash up, so that I would not have to look at myself and also because I had developed a strong aversion to all unnecessary efforts, because of the cold and, of course, because of my shoes. This bodily contraption, at least for me, was a source of great annoyance.

In general, the articles of clothing they provided for me at the concentration camp were unsatisfactory. They weren't very functional, and they had gross flaws. They also became sources of annoyance. All in all I can assert with certainty: they just didn't work. For instance, in the thin gray rain that was a permanent fixture with the change of seasons, our canvas outfits became stiff stovepipes, and our scarred skin tried to avoid a wet touch at all costs—all for naught, naturally. The convict's cape—which, I can't deny, they doled out conscientiously—was useless in this case; it was another bother, another wet layer. In my opinion the rough paper of the cement sacks, which Bandi Citrom, like many others, wore under his clothes, didn't provide a satisfactory solution either. They used it braving all danger, for such sins soon surfaced: a hit with a stick on the back, another on the chest, and the paper's noise soon made the sin manifest. If, on the other hand, it no longer rustles, then I ask you: What is the use of this new apparel turned to wet mush, which we can only throw away in secret?

But the most annoying articles of clothing were the wooden shoes. It all began with the mud. I have to say that my prior experience concerning it was insufficient. At home I had also seen mud. I had even stepped in it, naturally, but I could never imagine that mud would become our chief preoccupation, the threat of our lives. What it means to sink into it up to your ankles and then with great exertion to free your feet from it with a single smacking pull, only to immerse yourself again twenty to thirty centimeters further away—I was not prepared for all this, and any preparation would have been in vain. Well, the worst thing about the wooden shoes was that eventually their soles would break. We walked on suddenly thinning and rounding-up soles, and we rocked back and forth on those round soles in the manner of Johnny-jump-ups. In addition, in the spot where the sole had been, between the side and the very thin heel, a slit appeared that grew daily; through this small opening at each and every step cold mud and along with it, of course, tiny gravel and all sorts of sharp little bits would stream in unobstructed. In the meantime the side would have long ago rubbed your ankles raw and would have created numerous sores in the soft flesh underneath it. These sores in turn would keep oozing, and their ooze is sticky. Because of this, then, we were unable to liberate ourselves from our shoes after a while. They became unremovable; they stuck to our feet and were like new limbs, almost as if they had grown onto our feet. I wore these during the day, and I slept in them, if for no other reason than not to waste time when I had to jump up or down from my sleeping place two or three times at night, some nights even four times.

Nighttime was still somewhat okay. After some scrambling and sliding in the mud outside, somehow we managed to reach our destination by the light of the reflectors. But what could we do during the daytime when the same diarrhea attacked us during work, which, of course, invariably happened? In those situations one mustered all of one's courage, took off one's cap, and asked the guard for permission to go to the latrine, provided there was some facility nearby—some facility, that is, that the convicts were permitted to use. But assuming that there was a place, assuming that the guard was kind and gave his permission once or even twice—then, let me ask you, who would have the audacity, the blind determination, to dare to try the guard's patience a third time? Then all that remained was a mute struggle with clenched teeth and constantly trembling nostrils, until it was finally decided who would be victorious— one's body or one's willpower.

And as the final tool—expected or not, braved or partly avoided—there was always the beating. I had my share of this too, naturally, but no more and no less than the regular, average, everyday convict. I was like any other. In other words, I received as much of it as was customarily allotted in our camp, barring any personal misfortune or ill luck.

But as an exception to the above statement I have to confess that I experienced the latter only once, and not through an official, authoritative SS person, but through a fellow named Tout, who, I heard, was a soldier attached to some sort of shady work-supervisory organization. He was there and noticed—after I had made much noise and jerked so that you couldn't believe it—that I had dropped a sack of cement. In fact, all of our work groups received the rare order of cement-loading with great joy—and rightfully so, in my opinion. You bowed your head, someone placed a sack on your neck, and then you walked over slowly to a truck, where someone else took the sack off your neck. Then with a nice long detour, whose perimeters were only determined by the opportunity of the moment, you walked back slowly, and if you were lucky, there was a line waiting, giving you some more time until the next sack. Now the sack only weighed about ten to fifteen kilograms; judged by normal, at-home circumstances, this would be child's play. Indeed, I could even play ball with it. Here, however, I stumbled and dropped it. What made matters worse was that the paper broke and the insides, the material, the valuable, expensive cement, flew out of the chink and spread on the ground.

Then Tout was standing next to me, and I felt his fist in my face. When he had me on the ground, I felt his boots in my ribs and his hands on my neck as he kept pushing my face into the ground, into the cement. I had to pick it up, scrape it together, lick it up, he suggested irrationally. Then he jerked me up: "I want to show you, Arschloch, Scheisskerl, verfluchter Judehund" [asshole, shithead, damned dog of a Jew], so that I would never again drop a sack, he threatened. From that moment on, then, at every turn, he was the one who loaded the new sack on my neck. I was his only care; he had eyes only for me, following me with his glance to the truck and back and taking me as the first even when, according to justice, others should have preceded me. Toward the end we almost played together, got to know each other. I almost perceived a kind of satisfaction, encouragement—I would almost say a kind of pride—on his face, and, from a certain point, I had to admit, justifiably so: even if I meandered or bent over, even if I occasionally had visual blackouts, I persisted, I came and went, I carried and brought everything without dropping a single sack again. And in the final analysis I had to recognize that this proved him right. On the other hand, at the end of that first day I felt that some irreparable damage had been done to me; from that point on I was convinced that every morning would be the last morning I would wake up, that every step would be my last, that every move would be my last. Still, at least for the moment, I was able to go on.

There are some cases, one can find some situations, that no knowledge can make any easier to bear, it seems. I can say that after all those attempts, all those useless trials and exhaustions, after some time I also found peace, quiet, and relief. Certain things, for example, that I had previously considered tremendously, almost incomprehensibly important now lost all value in my eyes. At the muster, for instance, when I became exhausted and wasn't spotted, I simply sat down; even if there was mud or a puddle, I just sank down and stayed there until my neighbors dragged me up with force. Cold, wetness, wind, or rain no longer disturbed me. They couldn't reach me. I never felt them. Even my hunger vanished; I continued to lift to my mouth whatever I found, whatever was edible, but I did it absentmindedly, mechanically, from habit, one might say. At work? I was totally unconcerned about appearances. If I didn't meet with their approval, the most they could do was to beat me, though even then they couldn't really harm me. Even in this way I occasionally won. With the first blow I quickly plopped down on the ground. Then I felt nothing, because I immediately fell asleep.

Only one thing was strengthened in me: my irritability. If anyone reduced my momentary comfort, or even touched my skin, or if, for example, during a march I switched steps (which happened frequently) and someone behind me stepped on my heels, I could have killed that person on the spot, without any hesitation and without giving it any further thought—that is, if I had actually been able. I could not by that time lift my arms and usually forgot what I wanted to do.

I had a few words with Bandi Citrom. "You let yourself go," he said. I was a burden to the commander. I created problems for everyone. He was catching my skin rash, he claimed. But mainly I got on his nerves, disturbed and upset him in one particular detail. I noticed this when one night he made me go to the washing facilities. I resisted, struggled in vain; he took off my rags forcibly, and even as I tried to hurt his body and face with my fists, he rubbed my trembling skin with cold water. I told him a hundred times, "I don't want your care and concern. You should leave me alone, and go to hell!" "Do you want to rot here?" he asked. "Don't you want to go home?" I'm not sure which answer he read in my face, but on his face I saw shock, a type of panic we usually view in hopeless trouble-makers, the condemned, or, let's say, those who carry the plague. It was then that I remembered what he had said about the Muslims. At any rate, after this incident he steered clear of me, so that I was finally relieved of this burden too.

I couldn't be rid of my knee, however. It pained me constantly. A few days later I looked down at it, and even though my body was used to surprises, this burning red sack that the area around my right knee had become left me wanting to immediately cover it up to keep it from sight. I knew, of course, that there was a field hospital at our camp, but office hours were conducted at dinnertime, and on reflection I decided that dinner was more important than getting well. Furthermore, a few experiences and a knowledge of that place and of life in general didn't exactly build trust in one. In addition, it was far away—two tents ahead of us—and taking such a long journey, except when forced by absolute necessity, especially now that my knees were hurting so, was not appealing.

Finally Bandi Citrom and one of our sleeping mates carried me over on a seat formed like a swing by their hands, and then they placed me on the table and warned me well in advance: it is likely that it will probably hurt, because immediate surgery is unavoidable, and faced with a lack of anesthetics, surgery will have to be performed without it. What I could observe during the operation was that they made two cuts crosswise with a knife above my knee, through which they pressed out that sea of stuff that was in my thigh, and then they wrapped everything in paper. I immediately mentioned dinner, and they reassured me that necessary care would be taken, and I soon found out that this was indeed so. The soup that day was made of turnips and kohlrabi, which I find very tasty, and they measured out the sick-bay portions from the thick of the soup, which again pleased me. I spent the night there in the sick-bay tent on top of a box entirely by myself, and the only unpleasant event was that when the usual time for the diarrhea came, I couldn't use my own legs. I called—first whispering, then shouting loudly, and finally screaming—for help in vain.

The next morning, then, together with some other bodies, mine was thrown into the wet bin of an open truck and driven to a nearby locality, called Gleina, if I heard it right, where the camp hospital was located. In the back, sitting on a neat, folding footstool and with a shiny wet shotgun on his lap, a guard watched us on the journey with obvious resentment. His face was drawn, and at the inevitable sudden gust of an odor, he grimaced with clear disgust—and with some justification, I had to admit. What pained me most was that it seemed that he was forming an opinion, deducing some general truth, from this, and I felt like making excuses for myself: it wasn't entirely my fault; originally this was not my nature at all. But proving this to him would be nearly hopeless, I could see.

When we arrived I had to endure first the unexpected stream of water from some sort of garden hose that attacked me everywhere and washed off everything: the remaining shit, the filth, and also the paper bandages. Then they carried me to a room and issued me a shirt and put me into the lower level of a two-storied wooden bunk. Here I could lie down on a straw sack, presumably pressed down and flattened by my predecessor and here and there colored by suspicious stains and suspiciously smelly, suspiciously cracking discolorations. Still, the place was unoccupied, and they left me to my own resources to pass the time and finally to take a nice long nap.

Apparently we take our old habits along with us to new places. I can say that while I was in the hospital I initially had to fight off some old fixations and clinging habits. Take my conscience, for instance: in the first days, it woke me up exactly at dawn every day. At other times I woke up trembling. I had missed the call to muster. They were already starting the search, and only with a slowly quieting heart did I realize my mistake and accept the picture around me, a testimony to reality, as I felt that I was at home, that everything was okay. Someone was sighing over here, over there some people were talking, and somewhere else another person stared at the ceiling with a strange silence, a pointed nose, immobile eyes, and an open mouth. It was only my wound that was hurting, and at most I was thirsty—as always—presumably because of the fever. In other words, I needed a certain amount of time actually to believe that there was no mustering call, that I didn't have to face the soldiers, and, most of all, that I didn't have to go back to work. All of these advantages, for me at least, could not be fundamentally spoiled by any circumstances, any sickness.

Occasionally they took me upstairs to a little room where two doctors worked, a younger one and an older one. I was a patient of the latter, to be precise. He was a thin, black-haired, sympathetic person with a clean suit and shoes, with an armband and a distinguished face that reminded one of a friendly, aged fox. He asked me about my home and told me that he hailed from Transylvania. In the meantime he peeled off the tattered dressing around my knee—the invariably hardened greenish-yellow paper—and then, pushing with both hands, he pressed out from my thigh whatever had collected there between visits. Finally with an instrument resembling a crocheting needle he pushed a rolled-up piece of gauze between my bandage and my flesh, and he explained that this was to "keep the drainage going," for "the sake of the cleansing procedure," in order to prevent my wound from healing too quickly.

I liked to hear that, because, after all, I had no business elsewhere. As far as I was concerned, I was not in the least bit desirous of getting healthy. I liked another of his observations less. He thought that the one opening on my knee was not enough. He was of the opinion that we should have another cut on the side and connect it with the initial incision through a third cut. He asked me if I was willing, and I was amazed because he looked at me like someone who was indeed waiting for my answer, even my agreement. I told him, "Whatever you like." His judgment was that waiting was not good. He began the operation right there, right away, but I was forced to be rather loud, and that, I noticed, made him tense. He mentioned several times, "I can't work like this," and I tried to make excuses: "I can't help it." After making a few centimeters of progress, he finally gave in without completing his plan. Still, he seemed reasonably satisfied, and he said, "This, at least, is something," because now he could squeeze the pus from at least two places, he thought.

Time passed quickly in the hospital. When I was not sleeping, hunger, thirst, the pain around my wounds, an occasional conversation, or the events surrounding the treatment kept me occupied. But without any work to do, or, I should say, with this pleasant, spine-tingling thought, this forever and inexhaustible source of joy of not having any work to do, I felt great. I kept asking newcomers: What is the latest news from the camp? Which blocks were they from? And did they know a man from Block 5 by the name of Bandi Citrom, of medium height, broken-nosed, with teeth missing in the front? But no one could recall him. In the treatment room I saw wounds similar to mine, usually on the thighs or on the lower legs, though there were occasionally some further up on the hip, or more rarely on the arms, or even on the neck and the back. The scientific name for this condition was *phlegmon*, as I heard it often called. Its occurrence was not in the least unusual in a concentration camp, the doctors explained. Somewhat later, those whose feet needed all the toes or one or two cut off began arriving. In the camp in winter, people's feet froze in their wooden shoes.

At times an obviously high-ranking official in a custom-tailored prison suit entered the treatment room. I heard this soft, yet quite audible word from him: "Bonjour!" From that, plus the *F* letter in his red triangle, I quickly gathered that he was French, and from the *O. Arzt* inscription on his armband I realized that he must be the chief doctor of our hospital. I watched him for a long while because I hadn't seen such a handsome man in some time: he was tall, but his suit was filled out proportionately, and he had a lot of flesh attached tightly to his bones. His face was also filled out; every line on it was unmistakably his, with recognizable shades of emotions. His chin was round and had a dip in the middle, and his darkish, olive-colored skin reflected like satin in the light, just the way it had reflected back home, in the past, among his people.

I didn't judge him to be old. I guessed around thirty. I noticed that the other doctors became lively and tried to please him, to explain everything to him, and I also noticed that their manners were not camp manners, but the old ones from home, and in a way that was reminiscent of home they treated him with that joy, social grace, effort, and selectivity that we usually show when we speak and understand a cultured language like, for example, French. By contrast, I noticed that all this meant absolutely nothing to the chief doctor. He looked at everything; he answered a word here and there or nodded, but all this slowly, quietly, sadly, without caring one way or the other. On his face and in his nut-brown eyes was the unchanging expression of sadness, almost a depression. I was utterly amazed, because I couldn't understand what the cause could be in such a well-to-do, well-off official who had achieved such a high rank. I tried to search his face and follow his movements, and only gradually did I understand that he too was forced to be here. Only slowly, and not without some humorous puzzlement and wonder, did the idea dawn on me: this situation, this state of imprisonment, had to be what was causing his agony. I was almost tempted to say to him: "Don't be sad. After all, it's not important." But I was afraid to be so bold, and then I also remembered that I didn't know any French.

I slept through the next move. The news had reached me earlier: in place of the Zeitz tents, they had built some stone barracks for winter quarters, and among these they hadn't forgotten the hospital building. They loaded us onto some trucks again. Judging by the darkness, it must have been evening, and judging by the coldness at the bottom of the truck, it must have been midwinter. The next thing I noticed was the cold anteroom of a massive place, well lighted, with a wooden tub smelling of chemicals. I had to dip myself in this from head to toe for cleansing, in spite of all my pleading, begging, crying. This wooden tub caused me to shudder, not only because of the coldness of its contents but also because I saw that all the sick people were dipped in that same way, in the same brown liquid as me, wounds and all. Here too time began to pass basically as in the previous place, except for a few minor differences. In the new hospital, for example, the bunks were three levels high. That allowed us to see the doctor less frequently, so that here my wound cleansed itself more of its own accord. In addition, I soon began to have a pain on my left hip, and then there was the already-familiar burning red bag of pus. After a few days, while I waited in vain for it to disappear or for something else to happen, I had to say something to the male nurse, and after some repeated urgings and a few more days of waiting, it was my turn to see the doctor in the anteroom of the barracks. So I now had another approximately hand-sized incision on my left hip in addition to the one on my right knee.

Again, an unpleasant circumstance arose because of my place on one of the lower bunks opposite a tall glassless window that looked out onto an always-gray sky. On its iron bars were eternal icicles and constant, hairy snow flowers, which were caused presumably by the streaming breaths inside. I wore only the dress of the sick: a short, buttonless shirt and, as an admission of its being winter, a strange cap circling my ears and forehead, somewhat like the caps worn by ice-skating competitors or by actors playing the role of Satan on the stage. Other than that, it was a very useful green knitted cap.

In this way I was continually cold, especially after I lost one of my two blankets, whose rags I had until then used to supplement the shortcomings of the other cover. The attendant requested that I lend it to him for a short while; he'd return it soon. I tried in vain to grasp it with both my hands and to hold on to the end. He proved stronger, and aside from the physical loss, I was also partly pained by a thought: namely, that they usually remove the cover from those whom they expect to expire soon. At another moment an already-familiar voice warned me from a lower bunk to lie on my back. Again, an attendant must have made his appearance with a new patient on his arm, looking for an empty spot. The patient was entitled to a private bed because of the severity of his condition, and he thundered and shouted in an awful voice: "I object! I have a right to it!" and "Ask the doctor!" and then again "I object!" Then the attendants finally took their burden to another bed, namely, to mine, by virtue of which I ended up with a boy approximately my age for a bunkmate.

His yellow face, his large, burning eyes, seemed familiar. But then again, everyone here had yellow faces and large, burning eyes. His first words were for water, and I let him know that I myself wouldn't mind having a sip. His second request, following immediately on the heels of the first, was for a cigarette. Here too he was out of luck, of course. He offered me some bread in exchange, but I told him, "That's not it. That's not it at all. I just don't have any." Then he stopped speaking for a moment. My suspicion was that he was running a fever, judging by the heat unceasingly streaming from his trembling body—a heat that gave me a pleasant advantage.

I was less happy with his constant nighttime tossing and turning, showing little consideration for my own wounds. I finally told him: "Hey, lay off. Calm down. Go to sleep for a while," and finally he listened. Only in the morning did I notice why he had listened. I wasn't able to wake him for the morning coffee. Still, in a hurry, I handed his pot to the attendant, because just as I was getting ready to report my actions to him, he screamed at me, demanding the pot. Then I took his bread portion too, and I had his soup in the evening, until one day he began to behave very strangely. Then I was finally forced to speak up, because I could no longer maintain the situation in my bed that way. I was nervous, because my delay in reporting was quite noticeable and because I could assume that with only a little expertise the change in his condition could be easily detected. Still, he was carried out along with the others, and nothing, fortunately, was said. For the moment I was left alone, without any company.

Here I made the acquaintance of vermin, but I never caught any fleas. They were much faster than I was, because they were better nourished. I could easily catch the lice, but what was the sense in that? When they annoyed me, I randomly dragged my thumbnail down the stretched shirt on my back, and I could measure my revenge, enjoy the destruction, by the clearly audible puffs. I would repeat the procedure after a minute in the same spot with the same results. There was a swarm of them. They set up house in every nook and cranny. My green cap was gray with them and hummed. It almost vibrated with them.

Still, I was startled and taken aback when I observed a certain ticklish sensation on my hip, and on lifting the paper bandage I saw that they were already on my flesh, eating my wound.

I tried to shake them off, to free myself, to get rid of them at least here, to dig them out, to scratch them out, to force them at least to show patience, to wait. But I have to say, never have I felt a struggle to be more futile, never a resistance more stubborn than this. In time I yielded and just watched this gluttony, this eagerness, this greediness, this appetite, this undisguised bliss: certainly, it was as if I knew all this from somewhere else a little bit. Then when I began thinking of their behavior, I saw that I could to a certain degree understand them. Eventually I was almost relieved; my aversion almost disappeared. I still wasn't happy. I was still somewhat depressed, saddened, and not without reason, I think, but I was without anger, or angry only in a vague way just at that form of nature in general. At any rate, I quickly covered up the wound and no longer fought with them. I didn't disturb them any longer.

I can say one thing for certain: there is no degree of experience, no perfect resignation, no such power of recognition, it would seem, that can lead us to deny ourselves a final chance at good fortune—provided, of course, the occasion arises. So when, along with all those for whom work here was obviously rather hopeless, they returned me to sender, so to speak, to Buchenwald, I mustered all my remaining ability, naturally, to share in the joy of the others, because the good old days spent there and especially the morning soup immediately stirred my memory. What I didn't consider, however, and I admit it, was that first I'd have to travel there on the train under the usual circumstances of such trips. In any case, I can say there was a lot that I had never before understood and would probably not have believed anyway. Such a common expression, for example, as *earthly remains* until then only suggested a corpse. Yet as far as my living was concerned, I doubtless existed, even if I was only sputtering along with the flame turned entirely down. But still something within me burned—the flame of life, as they used to say—in other words, my body was still there. I was thoroughly familiar with it, only somehow I myself no longer lived inside it.

Without any difficulty I sensed that my body lay there surrounded on the sides and above with other objects. On the cold floor of the rattling railroad car the straw was wet from a variety of suspicious fluids. I sensed that my paper bandages had long since torn apart and disappeared, that my shirt and convict's pants, which they had put on me for the journey, were sticking to my wounds. But all this no longer moved me, no longer interested me, no longer held any sway over me. Indeed, I have to say that a lot of time had passed since I had experienced this easy, peaceful, and (to call a spade a spade) comfortable quiet. After all, I had finally become rid of the pain of irritability: the bodies pressing against mine no longer disturbed me. Somehow I was even glad that they were there with me, that their bodies and mine were so connected and so similar, and now for the first time I felt a strange, unusual, somewhat shy, almost clumsy feeling toward them. Perhaps it was love, I think. And I experienced the same from them as well, although they no longer encouraged me with hope as at the beginning.

Maybe this feeling—aside from other difficulties, naturally—was also responsible for making their talk so quiet and yet so familial that one could hear, aside from the general words, a hissing through the teeth and soft complaints: they were words of solace and calming. But I have to say too that those who were able didn't skimp on deeds either; so, for example, very dutifully many hands from I don't know how far passed the brass can when I announced that I had to urinate. And when finally a stone pavement and iced-over puddles were under my back instead of the floor of the boxcar—I don't know how, when, or by whose help—I have to say that I no longer cared that I had arrived at Buchenwald, and I had long since forgotten that this was the place I had yearned for so much. I had no idea where I was: at the train station or further along. I didn't recognize the area and didn't see the country houses or the statue that I still remembered so well.

At any rate, I must have lain peacefully, mildly, without curiosity, patiently, for a long time where they deposited me. I felt no cold and no pain, and it was my mind, not my skin, that registered the needlelike sensation of some kind of precipitation that was somewhere between snow and rain. I mused about this and that. I looked around at what came into my view without any need for effort or movement from me, as, for example, the low, gray, impenetrable sky passed above my face, or more precisely the slowly moving winter clouds covered up the sky. There were also occasional openings in the sky, an unexpected aperture here and there, and for a fleeting second a shiny hole; this was like the sudden suggestion of some depth from which a ray of light hit me from above, a quiet, inquisitive glance, an indefinitely colored eye, but doubtless made of light. It reminded me of the doctor who had once examined us at Auschwitz. Right next to me was a shapeless thing, a wooden shoe, and on the other side my eyes met a devil's cap like mine with two pointed appendages—a nose and a chin—and between them a sunken space. Beyond other objects and bodies, I ascertained the remnants of the cargo—its garbage, to speak more exactly—which they had presumably deposited here for a time. After a while—whether an hour, a day, or a year, I don't know—I finally made out some voices, noises, and the sound of work and organizing.

The head next to me was suddenly lifted, by the man's shoulders. I saw arms in his convict's suit as they prepared to throw him onto some sort of a cart, on top of a whole pile of previously collected bodies. At the same time a broken phrase reached my ears, which I could barely distinguish, and in this husky whisper I recalled a once-commanding voice: "I . . . ob . . . ject!" he mumbled. For a second there, before the arc of his flight was completed, he hung motionless in the air, as if surprised, I felt, and immediately I heard another voice, belonging presumably to the person who had held up his shoulders. It was a pleasant, manly voice, quite friendly, a little foreign-sounding, speaking camplike German. I felt that his voice showed a certain surprise, some sort of wonder rather than resentment as he asked: "Was? Du willst noch leben?" [What, do you still want to live?]. And indeed, I myself thought that this desire was strange, entirely unwarranted, and, all in all, rather pointless at the moment.

That's when I resolved that I myself was going to be more reasonable. But they were already bending over me, and I had to squint, because a hand was fiddling around my eyes before they popped me, too, into the middle of the load on a smaller cart and started to push me . . . where, I didn't much care to know. I was preoccupied with one single thought, one question that occurred to me at that time. Possibly it was all my fault that I lacked the answer, but I had never had enough foresight to inquire into Buchenwald customs, procedures, and habits. In other words, how did they do it here? With gas, as in Auschwitz, or perhaps with the help of medicine, as I had heard, or perhaps with a bullet, or who knew by what other means? There were a thousand possible ones, but I could not name them. I had no idea how it was going to be done. At any rate, I hoped that it wouldn't hurt. This may sound implausible, but this hope was just as genuine, as intense as any other hopes that (how shall I put it?) we attach to the future. And it was then that I realized that feeling of vanity that accompanies one to the very end, it seems, because truly, regardless of how the curiosity concerning this question gnawed at me, I offered no questions, no requests, not a single word. I didn't even cast a fleeting glance at him or them who were pushing us along.

The road carried us to a steep turn, and suddenly a wide panorama presented itself to my view. There it was: the mountainside densely covered with identical little stone houses, a neat lawn, and then a separate group of new and rather austere, as-yet-unpainted barracks, complete with a maze of inner winding wire fences separating the different zones, and further off a tremendous group of new, naked trees disappearing as they were swallowed up in the middle. I don't know why so many naked Muslims waited at one of the buildings in the company of a few officials walking up and down, and if I saw correctly—yes indeed, I did recognize them by their little stools—there were some barbers. So they must have been waiting for a bath and then admission. But further along, the cobblestoned camp streets were alive with movement, busyness, actions, and signs of people passing the time away—longstanding inhabitants, convalescents, dignitaries, storekeepers. The lucky members of the internal units were coming and going, attending to their daily chores. Here and there suspicious smoke mixed with more friendly vapors, and from somewhere the sound of a familiar clanging reached out to me, like the ringing of bells in one's dreams, and my roving glance found a marching group of men weighed down by soup pots carried on sticks, and in the air I recognized without a doubt the distant smell of turnip soup. That was a pity, because this view and the fragrance had begun to elicit a throbbing in my numb breast, whose growing waves succeeded in pressing out a few warm drops from my dried-out eyes to mingle with the cold moisture lying on them. And in spite of any other consideration, rational thought, feeling of resignation or of common sense, I still couldn't mistake the furtive words of some kind of quiet desire rising from within myself, as if embarrassed because of their senselessness, but yet consistently stubborn in their persistence: I would so much like to live a little longer in this beautiful concentration camp!

10

I have to admit that there is a lot I could never explain, not in any exact way, not if I tried to base my explanations on reason, not if I viewed events from the point of view of life in general and the usual order of things, at least in the way I had known it. So when I was unloaded from the cart somewhere onto the ground, I simply couldn't comprehend how to face razors or haircutters. That jam-packed room, which at first glance looked convincingly like a shower and onto whose slippery wooden floor they placed me along with a mass of sticky heels, feet, and abscessed calves, matched my expectations by and large. A thought passed through my head: "Well, well, so it seems that here they also use the Auschwitz method." My surprise was all the greater when, after a short wait and some bubbling, hissing noises, suddenly water—warm, generous amounts of water—began to gush forth unexpectedly from the pipes above. I was less delighted—since I would have enjoyed warming up a little longer, but of course, I was powerless to alter events—when suddenly some irresistible force threw me through the air away from the busy forest of legs, while some sort of sheet and then a blanket were wrapped around me. Then I remember a shoulder onto which I was thrust with my head facing backward and my legs dangling in front, a door, and the steep steps of a staircase, then another door and a place, I should say a room, where, in addition to spaciousness and light, the almost military splendor of the furniture and fixtures met my doubting eyes, and I finally recall the bed—a real, true, genuine, obviously one-person bed complete with a well-stuffed straw mattress and two gray blankets, onto which I was lowered by my shoulders.

I further recall two men—really beautiful men with faces, hair, white trousers, and T-shirts, wearing wooden clogs. I kept looking at them, feasting my eyes on them. They in turn were looking at me. Only then did I notice their lips and realize that for a while I had been listening to some sort of musical language. I had the feeling they wanted to learn something from me, but I could only shake my head: I couldn't understand. Then one of them asked, in a very strange accent, in German: "Hast du Durchmarsch?" That is, "Do you have diarrhea?" And with some surprise I noticed that my voice—I don't know why—responded, "Nein," I guess still out of vanity. Then after some consultation and some commotion, they pressed two objects into my hand. One was a pot with some lukewarm coffee, the other a piece of bread (in my estimate, about a one-sixth portion). I could take it, eat it, without any payment or exchange. Then my attention and even more so all my powers were totally occupied with the suddenly aroused signs of life from my intestines, which began to make disobedient noises. I mustered all my strength to prevent my insides from giving the lie to my earlier words. Then I was startled by the presence of one of the men, now dressed in boots, wearing a nice dark-blue cap and a convict's coat with a red triangle.

Up on his shoulders I went, then down the stairs, and straight out into the fresh air. Soon we entered a large gray wooden barracks that looked very much like a sanatorium or a sick bay, if I'm not mistaken. No denying it, here everything looked just about the way I expected it should, and in the final judgment, everything was perfectly acceptable and in order. Only I couldn't quite understand the previous treatment, the coffee, and the bread. As we shuffled along the barracks, a long row of familiar three-storied boxes greeted me. All were jammed full, and an experienced eye—which, I must say, I now possessed—could distinguish, in the middle of the flowers of disease and abscess, bones, and sharp joints, that in every compartment there were at least five or six bodies. In addition, I looked in vain for the portions of straw on the wooden planks that were allotted even in Zeitz, but for the short time that I presumably would have to remain there, I had to admit that this wasn't a very important demand.

Then followed another surprise: we had suddenly stopped, and the sound of a discussion struck my ears, presumably between the man carrying me and someone else. At first I couldn't believe my eyes, and yet I couldn't be mistaken, because the barracks were well lighted by strong lamps. To my left I saw two rows of regular boxes, but the planks were covered with a layer of red, pink, blue, green, and lilac coverlets, while above them was another layer of similar covers, and between the two layers, near each other, were the bold heads of children peeking out—some large, some small, but most approximately my age. Just as I was taking all this in, they lowered me, while someone propped me up so that I wouldn't topple over. They removed my blanket, quickly wrapped my feet and hip with a paper bandage, and then put a shirt on me. I was immediately slid into one of the rows with coverlets on top and bottom, and two boys on either side hurriedly made room for me on the second level.

Then they abandoned me without any explanation, so that once again I was left to my own resources to make sense out of things. At any rate, I had to admit that I was here, and this fact, which I couldn't deny, reinforced itself with every succeeding moment as this situation went on.

Later some other essential details became clear. This was probably the front of the barracks, not its back, as was suggested by the door opposite me that opened to the outside and also by the light, spacious area in front of me, which was furnished with a tablelike construction that was covered by a white sheet in the center and was usually surrounded by officials, secretaries, and doctors at work. Those who were housed in the back in the wooden boxes usually suffered from typhus or were soon expected to. The first sign—signaled by an unbearable smell—was diarrhea. It is also called *Durchfall* or *Durch-*

marsch; the men of the bath squad had asked me about it, and I knew I should have been entirely honest back there. Daily rations and the kitchen schedule were comparable to those of Zeitz: coffee came early in the morning, soup arrived at mid-morning, the portion of bread was one-third or one-fourth the usual size, and when the portion was one-fourth there was usually a supplement. I had difficulty telling the time of day because of the constant and never-changing lighting, which was not affected by the light or darkness of the windows. I could only tell the time by unmistakable signs such as the morning by the coffee and the time for sleep by the doctor's "good night."

I made the doctor's acquaintance the first evening. My attention was caught by a man who stood directly in front of our box. He could not have been very tall because his head was approximately on a level with mine. His face was not only full but also genuinely round and here and there even pudgy from excess; not only did he have an almost entirely gray mustache turned into a circle, but to my great amazement, since I had never experienced this in the concentration camp before, he also had a similarly gray, well-tended little beard, neatly shaped to a point on his chin. Along with all this he wore a very dignified cap and dark wool trousers. He still wore a convict's coat, although it was made of good material, with an armband and a red sign inscribed with the letter *F*. He looked me over as is customary with a newcomer, and he also spoke to me. I answered with the only sentence I knew in French: "Yö nö kompran pa, mösjö" [Je ne comprend pas, monsieur; I don't understand, sir]. "Oui, oui," he replied, with a booming, friendly voice, a little husky. "Bon, bon, mon fils" [Yes, yes. Good, good, my son]. Then he placed a piece of a cube of sugar in front of my nose on the cover—a real, true piece of sugar, of the kind that I remembered from home.

Then he visited all the other boys in both boxes, on all three stories, and they too received pieces of sugar from his pocket. With some of the boys he simply left the sugar, but with others he spent more time. There were some who were able to talk to him, and those he patted on their cheeks, tickled their necks, chitchatted, twittered with them during the hour allotted the way one twitters with one's favorite canary. I also noticed that for a few of his favorites, especially those who spoke his language, he found another piece of sugar. That's when I realized the truth of what they kept teaching me at home: what an important thing an education is, especially a knowledge of foreign languages!

All of this, as I said, I observed and grasped, but only with a queasy feeling, because all the while I kept waiting for I don't quite know what, for an answer to the puzzle, an awakening, one might say. The next day, for example, when the doctor seemed to have some time away from his other patients, he pointed to me with his finger. Then they pulled me out of my place and put me directly in front of him on the table. He released some friendly guttural noises, examined me, poked at me, put his cold ear and sharp little mustache against my chest and my back; he showed me how to breathe deeply and to cough. Then he had me lie flat on my back, and he asked some sort of an assistant to take off my paper bandages so he could look at my wounds. He examined them, at least from afar, then carefully touched the flesh around them, making something appear from inside. Then he hemmed and hawed, shaking his head. It seemed that this depressed him. Then he quickly wrapped them up again, as if to hide them from his eyes. I had to feel that these wounds were not in the least bit to his liking. He was very dissatisfied, quite displeased with them.

Then I was forced to see that some of my other exams turned out poorly too. One of my other problems was that I could not converse with the boys lying around me. They kept talking undisturbed above me, over my head, but in such a way as if my head were simply an obstacle to them. At first they asked who and what I was. I told them I was an "Ungar," and this word spread all over in many forms: *vengerski, vengrija, magyarski, matyar, ongrva*. One of them even said, "Khenyn" (that is, "bread"), and the way he laughed while saying it, accompanied by a chorus of laughter, left no doubt in my mind that he knew my kind quite well. It was unpleasant, and I wished that I could have told them: this is a mistake, because the Hungarians don't consider me one of them. Also to a great degree I shared the boys' views of them, and I found it strange indeed, even unfair, that here I was ostracized precisely because of them. But then I remembered the stupid obstacle of my only being able to explain all this to them in Hungarian or perhaps in German, which would even be worse, I figured.

There was also another fault, a continuing sin that, after all, I couldn't hide forever with any amount of willpower. I soon learned that on occasion, as my need arose, I had to call for a boy who was just a little older than I, some kind of assistant attendant. He would appear with a flat pan equipped with a handle, and he would place this under the blankets. Sometimes I had to call to him again: "Bitte! Fertig! Bitte!" [Please! Ready! Please!] until he brought it. As it was, no one, himself in-cluded, denied the rightful necessity of such a demand once or twice a day, but I was forced to bother him three times or even four times a day, and I could see that this annoyed him, quite understandably, to be sure. I couldn't deny that. Once he even carried the pot to the doctor and explained something, argued, and kept showing him the contents. The doctor studied the sinful signs a little, but judging by his gestures and the way he moved his head, he undoubtedly dismissed the charge. In the evening the piece of sugar wasn't omitted, and so I guessed that all was okay, and I firmly nestled myself between the un-shakable security of coverlets and warm bodies—at least for that day.

The next day, at some point between coffee and soup, a man entered from the outside world—one of those rare officials, as I knew immediately. His large artist's cap was made of black cloth; his clothes consisted of an impeccably pressed white coat, pants ironed to a sharp crease, shoes polished. I was frightened, though, by the lines on his face, which were some-how too manly, too rough, as if carved by a chisel, and also by the strikingly purple, almost freshly peeled appearance of his skin, which seemed to expose the raw flesh. Other than that he was tall and rounded, and his black hair was graying at the temples. I couldn't distinguish the inscription on his armband because his hands were folded behind him, but his letterless red triangle revealed flawless German blood and some sort of criminal activity. Incidentally, for the first time in my life, I was able to wonder at someone whose convict's number was not only not in the tens of thousands, or thousands, or even in the hundreds. It merely had two digits.

Our doctor hurried over to greet him, to shake his hand, to slap him on his arm, offering words to win his goodwill. He greeted him like a very welcomed guest whose visit had finally honored the household. To my great amazement I suddenly noticed that, without any doubt, he was talking about me. The doctor even pointed me out with a large arching motion of his hand, and from his quick, now German speech, an expression clearly struck my ears: "Zu dir" [to you]. Then he continued assuring the man, trying to convince him with a stream of words in the midst of explanatory gestures, the way one offers some merchandise for sale, trying to peddle it while also trying to jettison it as soon as possible. The man, after listening to our doctor wordlessly, looking like an unwilling buyer, eventually began to seemed convinced. At least that's what I felt from the short, piercing look of his small dark eyes glancing in my direction, which already assumed the look of a possessor, and from the short nod of his head, his handshake, and his whole way of behaving, and then from the cheerful, satisfied expression on our doctor's face as the man left.

I didn't have to wait long before the door opened again. With a glance I spied a newcomer in a convict's suit, with a red triangle with the letter P on it—which, as everyone knew, designated the Polish—and the word Pfleger [nurse] on his black armband. This had to be the dark-haired man's assistant. He seemed young, probably in his early twenties. He also wore a nice blue cap, though somewhat smaller. Underneath it his soft, chestnut-colored hair fell around his neck and ears. His longish but full, oval face was average-looking and very pleasant; his pink skin and the expressions on his rather large, soft lips were very appealing. In other words he was beautiful, and I certainly would have feasted my eyes on him for a long time if he had not immediately looked for the doctor, who, in turn, pointed me out to him. He had a blanket on his arm, and he wrapped me in it as soon as he pulled me out from under the covers and carried me, in what seemed to be the customary mode of transportation here, thrown over his shoulders. His job was not entirely easy, since I held on to the beam of the boxes with both hands, grabbing at it wildly, without thinking, one might say. I was a little embarrassed by the whole event. I understood then how our minds can be deceived and how all our affairs can be complicated by the experience of only a handful of days. Still, he proved to be the stronger, and I struggled in vain, trying to beat the section near his kidneys with both fists. He just laughed at me, as far as I could judge from the shaking of his shoulders. At that point I yielded and allowed myself to be carried wherever he wanted to take me.

There are some strange places in Buchenwald. Behind one of the barbed-wire fences you arrived at one of those neat green barracks that until now you were only able to admire from afar—that is, if you were a member of the little camp. Now you might discover that on the inside—of this one at least—there was a hallway gleaming and sparkling with suspicious cleanliness. Doors opened from the hallway—genuine, real, white doors—and behind one of these a warm, lighted room and a made-up bed awaited you, as if in expectation of your arrival. A red coverlet covered the bed. Your body sank into a well-stuffed straw mattress. Between you and the mattress—you could convince yourself that you were not mistaken—there was a cool barrier, indeed a sheet. You felt a pleasant, unfamiliar pressure under your neck: it was caused by a well-stuffed straw pillow with a white cover. The male nurse folded the blanket in which he had brought you four times and put it at your feet. That, it seems, was to assist you just in case you were dissatisfied with the temperature in the room. Then with some cardboard and a pencil he sat down next to the edge of your bed and asked your name. I told him: "64921." He wrote this down, but still he insisted—and it took a while until you comprehended—that he was also interested in your Name, and then again, it might take a while, as happened in my case, until, rummaging through your memory, you rediscovered it. He had me repeat it three or four times until he seemed to understand it. Then he showed me what he had written down, on the top of some ruled paper that looked like a fever chart. He asked me in Polish if it was *dobro jes* (that is, "good"), and I told him in German, "Gut." After putting the chart on the table, he left.

Then, since obviously you now had some time, you might look around, observe, even orient yourself a little. You might notice, for instance, if it hadn't struck you before, that some other people were also in the room. You only needed to glance at them to discover that they were also sick. You might guess that this color, this visual impression caressing your eyes, this sort of dominating, dark-red glow was really the reflecting color of the lacquered wooden-plank floors. And of course the coverlets on all the beds also had that same color. There were approximately twelve beds. All were single beds, and only those on my side against the white-painted, wooden separating wall and two on the opposite wall were two stories high. You gazed in amazement at the mass of unused space, at the large, comfortable, over-a-meter-wide spaces between the rows of beds, and you were totally baffled by the great luxury of one or two empty beds. You might also discover the extremely neat glass window divided into small panes that provided some light, and your eyes might discover the light brown stamp on your pillowcase depicting a hooked, beaked eagle, and you might be able to decipher the letters "Property of the SS."

You would be foiled, however, if you tried to examine the surrounding faces for a sign, some sort of statement concerning the event of your arrival, which, after all, you assumed had to be somewhat newsworthy. You might look for interest, disappointment, joy, annoyance, or anything, even just passing curiosity—all in vain. You would be suddenly faced with a silence that was more uncomfortable, more disturbing—I would almost say more mysterious—the more profound it became. This you'd experience as undoubtedly your strongest impression if by some odd chance you should end up here somehow. In a square space bordered by the beds stood a small table covered with a white cloth, and on the opposite side was a larger one with some chairs surrounding it. Next to the door you might see a large, ornate, well-stuffed iron stove and a shiny black coal container next to it.

And then you might start racking your brain: What were you to make of all this—the room, the joke, the coverlet, the beds, the silence? A lot might enter your mind, and so you would try to remember, to draw conclusions, to lean on your experience and knowledge. It is possible that you might conclude, as I did, that this is the sort of place I had already heard about in Auschwitz, where they feasted their patients on milk and honey until piece by piece they removed all their organs for the sake of knowledge and science. But of course one had to admit that that was simply one hypothesis, one out of many possibilities, and besides, I saw no signs of milk and honey. Furthermore, as I remembered, at the other place it was long past soup time, and here I saw no signs, heard no noise, smelled no smell to this effect. And so a thought entered my head, perhaps a dubious thought. But who can judge what is possible or believable in a concentration camp? Who could explore, exhaust all those countless ideas, inventions, games, jokes, and ponderable theories, which are easily accessible and transferable from a make-believe world of fantasy into a concentration-camp reality? You couldn't, even if you mustered the totality of your knowledge. Now then, I mused, you were carried into such a room. Suppose you were placed in a nicely covered bed like this. They cared for you, nursed you, made every effort to please you. Only, let's say, they didn't give you anything to eat. If this interested you, then it was worth wondering about who died and how all this had to have its own interest, maybe even its higher scientific usefulness. Regardless of how I approached the subject, the idea became more and more feasible and possible. And so, I thought, it could have occurred to someone who was far more knowledgeable than I.

I examined my neighbor carefully, the patient who lay just to my left. He was oldish and a little bald. His face still retained some of its original lines, and here and there, there was even some flesh. I also noticed that his ears looked suspiciously like the wax leaves of artificial flowers, and I recognized very well the yellow color of the tip of his nose and the area surrounding his eyes. He lay on his back, his cover moving with a gentle rising and falling; he seemed to be asleep. At any rate, just to experiment, I whispered, "Do you know Hungarian?" Nothing, no answer. He seemed not only uncomprehending but also deaf. I had turned away from him and was preparing to allow my thoughts to wander further, when a whisper, but still a word, unexpectedly reached my ears: "Yes." He had spoken, without a doubt, even though he neither opened his eyes nor altered his position. I, however, was so foolishly overjoyed (I'm not certain why) that I totally forgot for a few minutes my initial question. I added: "Where are you from?" He answered, after a pause that seemed interminable: "Budapest." I asked: "When?" After some patient waiting I learned, "In November." Then I finally asked: "Do they feed you here?" Again, after the necessary passage of time that for some reason he needed, he answered: "No." I was going to ask . . .

But at that moment the nurse again entered and went directly over to him, pulled back the cover, and wrapped him in his blanket. I was amazed at the ease with which he flung him over his shoulders and carried him out the door, even though, I noticed, his body was heavy. A piece of a paper bandage from around his stomach waved, as if to say good-bye. At the same time there was a short, sharp noise and then an electrical disturbance. Then a voice on the intercom said: "Friseure zum Bad, Friseure zum Bad," that is, "Barbers to the bath." It was a husky but quite pleasant, almost flattering voice, soft and melodious—the type whose eyes you almost feel upon yourself. On first hearing, it almost threw me out of bed. But for the other patients, this event elicited about as much excitement as my earlier arrival, so I assumed that this was also a customary event here.

I discovered a kind of loudspeaker above the door to the right, a brown box, and I also figured that apparently the soldiers received their orders through this machine. A short while later the attendant returned, again heading for the bed next to me. He placed the cover and the sheet back on the bed. He reached in for the straw mattress, and from his straightening and fluffing things up I understood: I will never see my neighbor again. I couldn't control my imagination's wondering if this, perhaps, was a punishment for divulging the secret and whether—after all, why not?—somehow through some machine similar to our loudspeaker, I don't know how, they had eavesdropped and perhaps heard? But then my attention was captured by another voice, belonging to a patient three beds down from me in the direction of the window.

He was a thin, young, white-skinned patient, with hair remaining on his head—thick, blond, and wavy. Two or three times he said, or rather moaned, the same word, elongating the syllables. It was a name that I was gradually able to distinguish: "Pjetyka! . . . Pjetyka!" In response the attendant spoke one word, similarly elongated and, it seemed to me, in a very warm tone: "Co?" [What?] Then the boy said something more elaborate, and then "Pjetyka." I guessed this was the attendant's name, since he went over to the boy's bed. For quite a while he whispered into the boy's ear the way we try to talk courage into a person, urging him to show just a little more patience, a little more endurance. While speaking, he reached behind the boy, lifted him up a little, and straightened out his pillow and cover, all in such a friendly, hearty, loving manner that it completely confused—almost contradicted—my former assumptions. The expression on the patient's face while leaning back I could only interpret as a kind of relaxation, a relief. The quiet, moaned yet clearly audible words "Gyinkuge . . . gyinkuge bardzo" [Thank you, thank you very much] were words of thanks, if I was not mistaken.

My cold, rational pondering was completely upset by an approaching noise and later an unmistakable clash filtering into here from the hallway, which stirred my whole being and filled me with a gradually growing and progressively less repressible longing, so much so that it made me forget any difference between my gaping preparedness and myself. Out there was a noise, coming and going, the clash of wooden spoons and then the sudden impatient shout of a thick voice: "Zal zeks! Essnhola!" That is, "Saal sechs! Essenholen!" or "Room 6! Bring in the food!" The nurse stepped outside, and then with the help of someone, whose arm I caught a glimpse of in the open doorway, he lugged in a heavy pot, and immediately the room was filled with the aroma of soup. Today it might be that same old dead vegetable soup. But I was mistaken on this count as well.

Later I observed more—the passing of the hours, the time of the day, and then the days themselves—and a lot became clear. At any rate, after a while—even if only gradually, carefully, and step by step—I had to accept the reality of the present events. I had to accept, it seemed, that this place was also possible, believable in a concentration camp, even if it was much more pleasant, of course. Still, I came to think, this place is no stranger, really, than all the other strange possibilities, one way or another, good or bad, in a concentration camp. On the other hand, this place disturbed me, made me uneasy, and undermined my sense of security. After all, if I examined it logically I could see no reason for its being, nothing rational or familiar. I could find no acceptable reason for finding myself here instead of somewhere else.

Gradually I discovered that all the patients here wore bandages, unlike those in the previous barracks, and so with time I ventured the hypothesis that the place over there was perhaps something like a section of internal examination, while this one (who knows?) might be the surgical department. Still, I couldn't consider this a sufficient reason, of course, or an acceptable explanation for all the work and trouble, the truly harmonious chain of hands, shoulders, thought, and planning that, as I studied it, had brought me from the wheelbarrow over there to this room, to this very bed. I tried to examine the patients, to figure them out a bit. In general, I noticed that they seemed to be mostly the older, indigenous inhabitants of the camp. I didn't consider any of them officials; on the other hand, I couldn't compare them with the Zeitz convicts either.

I was also eventually struck by the visitors, who were always coming for a minute or so at the same hour in the evening to exchange a word or two. They all wore red triangles, and I didn't see a single green or black triangle (a fact that I didn't miss) and what's more (and this I *did* miss) not even a yellow triangle. In other words, they were other people in blood, language, and age, but even beyond that, they were different from me or for that matter from the others whom until now I had understood quite well (and with whom I was getting along quite well), and all this puzzled me a bit. On the other hand, I had to feel that the explanation of this strangeness might lie precisely in this difference.

Take Pjetyka, for example. We went to sleep with his *dobra noc* [good night], and we woke up with his *dobre rano* [good morning]. The impeccable ordering of the room, the wiping of its floor with a wet rag attached to a stick, getting the coal every day, heating, apportioning the food, washing pots and spoons, and, when needed, transporting the sick and who knows what else—all this was the work of his hands. Even if he was a man of few words, his smile and his willingness to help were always the same: in a word, it was as if he wasn't the bearer of some important rank—after all, he was the room's foremost citizen and dignitary—but just a person who was primarily intent on serving the sick, since *Pfleger* was indeed written on his armband.

Or take the doctor—because, as I discovered, the rough-looking man was a doctor, in fact the chief doctor. His visits were part of the regular, unchangeable rituals of every morning. No sooner was the room made ready and our coffee drunk and the utensils hidden behind the blankets serving as curtains, where Pjetyka kept them, when we heard some familiar steps in the hallway. The next minute a determined hand opened the door wide, and the doctor entered with a *Guten Morgen* [Good morning] greeting, of which, however, only a drawn-out

Moogn was audible. For whatever reason, it was not appropriate for us to answer, and he didn't expect it, except perhaps from Pjetyka, who received him with his typical smile, bareheaded and looking respectful. As I observed several times during an extended period of time, however, he received the doctor not with that kind of familiar respect that we usually owe to those who outrank us, but rather somehow as if he actually did respect him of his own accord, for reasons of his own, so to speak.

Then the doctor lifted the charts one by one from the white table that Pjetyka had arranged there and examined them carefully and earnestly, entirely as if these were genuine charts in a genuine hospital, where there is no more important and obviously weighty question than the state of the patient's well-being. Then, turning to Pjetyka, he made one or two comments on some of them, but for him to respond or to give any sign of our presence, I quickly learned, was just as inappropriate as for us to reply to his "Good morning." He might then say "Der kommt heute 'raus!" This, I noticed, invariably meant that the respective patient was to go to see him that morning, either on his own two feet or on Pjetyka's shoulders, in his office, which was approximately ten or fifteen meters from the exit of our hall and was full of knives, scissors, and paper bandages. He, incidentally, unlike the doctor at Zeitz, didn't ask for my permission and wasn't disturbed by my loud objections as he cut two more openings into my hip with one of his strange-looking scissors; but from the fact that he then pressed out all of my wounds, padded them, lined them with gauze, and finally very carefully smeared a small amount of cream into them, I had to acknowledge immediately his professional competence.

His other occasional observation, "Der geht heute nach Hause," on the other hand, meant that he considered a patient already healed and ready to go *nach Hause,* that is, home, back to his camp block, to his work, his squadron. The next day everything happened the same way again, according to the exact rules of the same plan, in which Pjetyka, we patients, and even the pieces of furniture seemed to partake with equal seriousness, all playing our allotted roles, repeating this unchanged daily routine—strengthened by the practice, validating it, so to speak. In other words, we acted as if nothing were more natural or unquestionable than the fact that the doctor's very obvious concern and his only aim was to heal us, while ours was a speedy recovery, the quick regaining of our strength and a return home.

Later on I learned something else about him. It sometimes happened that there was a great deal of traffic in his office, since other people were also there. In such cases Pjetyka lifted me off his shoulders and placed me on a little bench to the side. There I had to wait until the doctor called me with a cheerful "Come, come, come, come!" With a probably friendly but still not particularly pleasant gesture, he grabbed me by my ears, pulled me toward the table, and lifted me on it with a single movement. At other times I found myself in the middle of all kinds of hustle and bustle with nurses carrying and moving patients, with ambulatory patients walking in; the room was filled with doctors and attendants working, and it was possible that I would be treated by another lower-ranked doctor, more modestly to the side, away from the main table in the middle of the room. I became acquainted with (I could even say I made friends with) one of them: a rather short, gray-haired, somewhat predatory-nosed man, who also wore an unmarked red triangle, and even if his number did not have two or three digits, it was still a very dignified number, in the thousands. He mentioned, and Pjetyka later confirmed, that our chief doctor had spent twelve years in the concentration camp: "Zwölf Jahre im Lager," he said quietly, nodding with a face expressing wonder at this rare and not altogether likely, but in his view at least incredible accomplishment. I asked him, "Und Sie?" [And you?] "Oich" [Me too], he answered, with his expression immediately changing. "Seit sechs Jahren bloss," "but only for six years," and he dismissed this with a single wave of his hand, as though it was some insignificant, trivial thing not worth mentioning.

Actually it was he who asked me how old I was, how I had ended up here so far from home. And that is how our exchange of ideas started. "Hast du was gemacht?" "Did you do something bad, maybe?" he asked, and I told him, "Nichts," no, nothing whatever. Then why had I ended up here? he wanted to know, and I told him for the very same reason that others of my kind had. But still, he asked stubbornly, "Why were you taken prisoner?" *verhaftet* [arrested], and I tried to explain to him briefly, as well as I could, about that particular morning, that bus, the customhouse, and later the military policemen. "Ohne dass deine Eltern?" that is, "Without the knowledge of your parents?" he wanted to know, and I told him, yes, *ohne*, "without, naturally." He seemed perplexed, as if he had never heard of such a thing, and I thought to myself, "Well, you must have been hiding from the world for six years, I think."

He immediately passed on the information to the doctor working next to him, and he, in turn, told the other doctors, the attendants, and the better patients. Finally I found myself surrounded by people shaking their heads and looking at me with peculiar expressions on their faces, which made me feel a little uneasy, because it seemed that they felt sorry for me. I had an urge to tell them: "There isn't any need, because, after all, right now at least." But still, somehow I couldn't say anything. Something held me back from speaking up. I just didn't have the heart to follow through. I felt that somehow they felt good about, even received some pleasure from, this feeling of sympathy. Maybe I was mistaken, but I didn't think I was. At other times when they asked me questions, interrogated me, I had the impression that they were actually exploring the opportunity to find a way, an excuse, for feeling this emotion, looking for some reason, some need of a proof of something, perhaps of the fact—who knows?—that they were still capable of feeling sympathy. At least this is how I sized up the situation. Then they glanced at each other in such a way that I looked nervously to see if we weren't being observed by some outsiders; but all I could see were the same foreheads with earnest shadows, narrowing eyes, mouths turned into lines—as if they had once again recalled something, as if something was once again confirmed in their eyes, and I had to think that it might have something to do with the reasons why they themselves were here.

Take the visitors, for example. I watched them too and tried to surmise how the wind could have blown them this way, what their business was. Initially I noticed that they came mostly in the evening, usually at the same time each day. Then I understood that here in Buchenwald there had to be an hour, as there was in Zeitz, between the return of the work squads and the evening muster. Most visitors had the letter *P*, but I also saw *J*, *R, T, F, N*, and even *No*, and who knows what else? At any rate, I have to say that I had some very interesting experiences and learned a lot through them, and through them I won some exact insights into the circumstances here, the conditions, the social life, so to speak.

The older inhabitants at Buchenwald were almost beautiful: their faces were full, their gestures and movements were quick, many were permitted to grow their hair, and they usually wore their convicts' clothes only for daily wear and tear, for work, as I noticed with regard to Pjetyka. He too, when he was preparing for a visit in the evening, after he had distributed our evening portion of bread (the customary third or fourth on certain days and the additional supplement on certain days), put on a shirt or a sweater, and with an expression of visible delight on his face and with movements he seemed to try to camouflage before us patients, he chose a pastel-colored, striped, fashionable suit from his wardrobe, whose only flaws were a square cut mended with something from a convict's suit, two long lines of red oil stains on the sides of the pants, and, of course, the customary red triangle on his chest and left pants leg, as well as the convict's number.

I found some unpleasantness (I would even say, a kind of temptation) when he was preparing to receive an evening guest. The arrangement of the room was responsible for a particularly unfortunate situation. For some reason, the wall outlet happened to be at the foot of my bed. And so, regardless of how I tried to occupy myself by staring at the flawless white of the ceiling and the enameled skirt of the lamp, in burying myself in my thoughts, eventually I had to recognize the fact that Pjetyka was squatting with his pot and his privately owned electric range. I had to listen to the sizzling of the warming margarine, had to breathe in the fragrance of the roasting onion slices and the slices of potatoes on top of them and then, perhaps, the impertinently persistent smell of the cut-in pieces of the supplemental sausage. On another occasion my attention was caught by a light, peculiar clink followed by a suddenly growing sizzling noise that—so my quickly averted yet amazedly starry eyes informed me—was caused by an object that was yellow in the center and white on the outside: an egg.

Then, when everything was ready and cooked, the dinner guest arrived. "Dobre vecser!" said Pjetyka with a friendly nod, because the visitor was also Polish. I heard that his name was Zbisek, but at other times, either because of inflection or as a term of endearment, Pjetyka called him Zbiskn. He held the position of attendant in another room somewhere beyond. He too arrived all dressed up, with boots and a blue flannel jacket appropriate for sports or hunting, although his back was also patched and he also had his convict's number on the front, while underneath it he wore a black turtlenecked sweater. He was tall and well built; his head was shaven, either out of necessity or by choice. I found him quite pleasant, a nice person with a cheerful, foxy expression on his fleshy face, even though I had no desire to exchange Pjetyka for him.

Then they sat down at a larger table in the rear, ate their dinners, and conversed while some of the Polish patients in the room occasionally contributed a quiet word here and there as an observation. Or they cracked jokes and put their elbows on the table, joining their hands in a trial of strength, the result of which, to the great delight of the whole room, myself included, naturally, was that Pjetyka usually succeeded in forcing Zbisek's arm down on the table, even though Zbisek's arm seemed stronger when one looked at it. I understood that the two of them shared all the advantages and disadvantages, the joys and the trouble, all the adversity here, and obviously even their wealth and daily portions of food. In other words they were friends, as the saying goes.

Besides Zbisek, others occasionally came to exchange a word or an object, and even though I could never see for certain what the object was, actually everything was clear, and I could easily understand everything, of course. Others also came to see one or another of the patients, quickly, furtively, almost as if in secret. For a minute or so they sat at the bedsides; at times they brought little packages wrapped in some awful paper and placed them on the blanket very modestly, even apologetically. And then, even though I couldn't hear their whispers and, even if I had heard them, I wouldn't have understood them, it was as if they were asking: "How are you doing, what's new?" and then they'd inform the sick about what was happening out there. They'd tell them that so and so was asking how you are doing and sends his greetings, and then they'd assure him that they'd pass on his greetings: "Yes, we won't forget." Time would pass, and slapping their arms on their friends' shoulders, as if to say, "Don't worry, we'll be coming again," they left, quickly and furtively and usually with contented looks on their faces. Other than that, they left without any success, advantage, or tangible profit, from what I could tell, and so I had to assume that the sole purpose of their visits was to exchange a few words, and nothing more, with their sick friends.

In addition, even if I wasn't aware of it, the brevity of their visits indicated that they were doing something prohibited that they could only do presumably by Pjetyka's turning a blind eye toward them. What's more, I suspect (and after long experience I'd even say it outright) that it was precisely this risk, this independence, this (I could almost say) stubbornness that was somehow a part of the whole event. At least that's what I deduced from the difficult-to-define but somehow cheerful expressions on the faces of the quickly departing visitors, because they had successfully broken some rules. It was as if they had succeeded in somehow changing, chipping away a little, damaging the established order, the sameness of the day-to-day existence or perhaps even Nature herself. That's, at least, how it appeared to me.

I saw the strangest people, however, far away from me at the bed of a patient on the opposite wall. Once at midmorning Pjetyka had carried him in on his shoulders and busied himself about him. I noticed that this case had to be serious, and I also heard that he was Russian. In the evening, half of the room was filled with visitors. There were a lot of *R*'s, but I also saw other letters, fur caps, and strangely padded pants. I saw some people, for instance, whose heads were shaved entirely on one side but not on the other. Others had normal hairdos except that a strip from their foreheads to their necks was shaved clean, the breadth of a razor. I saw coats with the customary patches and two intercepting red lines; they looked just like when we cross out an unnecessary letter, number, or sign from our writing. On other backs, large red circles with fat red center dots flashed from afar invitingly, temptingly, like targets, teasing you, signaling something to you: this is where you aim when you shoot, when the occasion comes. There they stood, shifting their weight from one foot to the other, discussing quietly among themselves. One bent down to straighten out the man's pillow. Another, it seemed, tried to catch the man's eye or get a word from him. Then suddenly I glimpsed something yellow. From somewhere they had brought out a knife and with Pjetyka's help a mug. There was the sound of a metallic squash, and even though I refused to believe my eyes, my nose brought me the incontestable proof that this yellow object—there could be no doubt—was, indeed, a lemon.

Then the door opened again, and I was flabbergasted, because now the doctor rushed in. I had never before seen this event at such an unexpected time. They cleared a path for him to walk to the bed, and he bent over the patient to examine him. He briefly felt something with his hands and then immediately departed with a severe (I'd almost say acerbic) look on his face, without having spoken a single word to anyone or cast a single glance at anyone. What's more, he even seemed to try to avoid the looks aimed in his direction. At least that was my impression. A little later I noticed that a strange hush descended over the visitors. One by one they stepped over to the bed and bent over the man, and then they began to leave, singly or in pairs, the way they had come. But now they looked broken, a little more awkward, a little more tired. I myself felt sorry for them at that moment, because I recognized that it was as if they had finally lost a hope that was also unreasonable, had lost a confidence, however secret. After a while Pjetyka very carefully lifted the man onto his shoulders and carried the corpse away.

Then, finally, there was the appearance of my friend. I met him in the bathroom. I had gradually grown accustomed to washing myself either in the bath at the end of the hallway or to the left at the water spigot, which could be turned on and off over a washbasin. Here I didn't wash because I was forced to, but because it was the proper thing to do, as I knew. With time, I noticed (and I almost resented) that the place was unheated, that the water was cold, and that there were no towels. Here you could also find a red portable toilet whose bowl was cleaned by I don't know who.

On one occasion, just as I was preparing to leave, a man entered the room. He was handsome, with straight black hair combed back but still unruly and falling onto his forehead on both sides. He had the almost greenish skin of some very darkhaired people. By his age—well into manhood—his wellgroomed appearance, and his snow-white coat, I would have taken him to be a doctor, had it not been that his armband identified him as merely an attendant, and the T in his red triangle as a Czech. He stopped and looked surprised, even seeming a little taken aback at the sight of me. That's how he stared at my face and my neck, which were sticking out from my shirt, and at my collar bones and my calves. He asked me something, and I answered from what I had picked up from the Polish conversations around me that I did not speak the language. Then he asked me in German who I was and my nationality. I told him that I was Hungarian and came from Room 6. Then he replied, using his pointing finger for explanation: "Du—warten hier. Ik: wek. Ein Moment zurück. Verstehen?" [You—wait here. I'm going away. Be back in a moment. Understand?]. I said sure, I understood. He left, and when he returned I found myself in the full possession of one-fourth of a piece of bread and a small, neat, already-open tin full of untouched, rosy chopped meat. I looked up to thank him, but all I could see was the door closing behind him. When I returned to my room and tried to let Pjetyka know what had happened and to briefly describe the man, he immediately informed me that he was the attendant from the next room, Room 7. He also mentioned his name: Bausch, I think, but on second thought maybe it was Bohus. This is how my neighbors pronounced it later—because in the meantime the patients continued to change.

Above me, for example, after having already removed someone the first afternoon, Pjetyka placed another person soon afterward, who was my age and my race but who spoke Polish. Pjetyka and Zbisek pronounced his name as Kuhalski or Kuharski, always stressing the *harski* part. Occasionally they joked around with him and probably teased him a bit or annoyed him, maybe because the boy was a little mad, judging by his quickly rattling tongue and the annoyed vibrations of his thickening voice, as well as the shower of straw that came down from his mattress through the separating planks. Everyone in the room who was Polish seemed to have great fun at his expense.

Someone now occupied the bed next to me, too, where the Hungarian patient had lain. He was a boy, but at first I couldn't quite figure out where he came from. He conversed easily with Pjetyka, but still my now-expert ear didn't quite accept this as Polish. His lack of response to my Hungarian words, along with his already-sprouting red hair, his rather full-featured but plain-looking face with its scattered freckles, and his blue eyes that seemed to size up and figure out everything quickly, made him look somewhat suspicious. While he settled in and made himself comfortable, I noticed some blue lines on his wrist, numbers from Auschwitz. His number was in the millions.

Only when the door suddenly opened one morning and Bohus entered to place his customary weekly or biweekly donations of bread and canned meat on my cover and leave according to his habit without waiting for thanks, just nodding in Pjetyka's direction, did I get to know that he understood at least as much Hungarian as I did, because he asked me at that moment: "Who was that man?" I told him that to my knowledge he was the attendant from next door, a certain Bausch, and that's when he corrected me. "Maybe Bohus," because, so he claimed, that was a very common name in Czechoslovakia, his homeland. I asked, "Why didn't you speak any Hungarian until now?" and he answered that that was because he disliked Hungarians. I confessed that he had a point and that generally I found little reason for liking them either. Then he suggested that we should converse in the language of the Jews, but I had to confess that I didn't understand it, so after all was said and done, we still ended up speaking Hungarian.

He told me his name: Loiz or Lojiz (I couldn't quite make it out). I said, "That's Lajos," but he objected vehemently because that was a Hungarian name, and he was Czech, and he insisted on the difference: Loiz. I asked him how he had learned so many languages. It was then that he told me he was originally from the Upper Region, from where the Hungarians had fled to avoid the "Hungarian occupation," together with their families, in-laws, and droves of acquaintances. Indeed, I then recalled a day in the distant past at home when flags, music, and day-long festivities announced that the Upper Region belonged once again to Hungary. He had ended up in a concentration camp, coming from a place named Terezín. He added, "You probably know it as Theresienstadt." I told him I didn't know it by either name, which surprised him greatly, just as I am surprised at people who, for example, haven't heard of the Csepel customhouse. Then he enlightened me: "It's the Prague ghetto." As he told me, he could also converse with— aside from Hungarians and Czechs and, of course, Jews— Germans, Poles, Ukrainians, and, if necessary, Russians. We then became very good friends, and I told him, because he was curious, how I had met Bohus, about my first experiences, my impressions, my thoughts on the first day concerning the room. He found these so interesting that he translated them for Pjetyka, who had a good laugh at my expense. I also let him know about the fear I had about the dying Hungarian patient. He translated Pjetyka's answer that the event was inevitable and that the patient's death just happened to coincide with my arrival by the merest chance. He said a lot of other things, but one thing made me a little tense: he prefaced every sentence by *ten magyar*, that is, "that Hungarian." But I thought Pjetyka sort of ignored that phrase, fortunately.

I also noticed, even though I made little sense of it, how he was usually occupied with time-consuming outside activities. I only began wondering when, on one occasion, he returned with some bread and canned meat—obviously goods derived from Bohus. But nothing surprised me, I have to admit. He let me know that he had chanced to run into Bohus in the bathroom, as I had. He had been spoken to also, and all the other details were identical with my experience. He, however, had been able to converse with Bohus; they discovered that they hailed from the same country, and this fact delighted Bohus. This was, after all, perfectly natural (so he said), and I felt compelled to agree. All this, when I viewed it rationally, became perfectly understandable, clear, and obvious, and I also held the same opinion that he held, which became apparent from the little observation he added to his account: "Don't be upset with me for stealing your man."

In other words, the assumption was that from this time forward, everything that I had been getting would now be his, and I would have to watch him eat the same way that he had been watching me. I was very surprised by this, but barely a minute later Bohus suddenly burst through the open door and headed directly for me. From that time on his visits were to us both. Sometimes he'd bring a portion for each of us, at times one for the two of us, according to his supplies, I guess. But in the latter case he never forgot to remind us with a determined gesture to share the portion in a brotherly way. He was always in a hurry and wasted little time with words; his face was compressed into a thoughtful, often worried expression, and occasionally he even had an annoyed look, as if he was someone whose shoulders were suddenly weighed down by a double load, by a double responsibility, but someone who was incapable of doing anything beyond bearing his fate patiently. I suspected that he received some pleasure from his actions and that this was his sole reason for doing them. It seems that his activities somehow satisfied a personal need, because I for one could think of no other reason for them, especially considering the scarcity of the merchandise and its market value and the intense demand for it. Regardless of how much I considered, pondered, and questioned myself, I could think of no other reason. And that's when I finally came to a general understanding of these camp people (at least I thought that I did). Because applying all of my experience and knowledge, linking the parts of the chain together left me without a single doubt: their behavior showed some kind of stubbornness, even if I was more familiar with other, more common types. Maybe it was a more traditional form of stubbornness, but to my knowledge it worked best, and above all, it was the most beneficial for me, without any doubt.

I can assert one thing: with time one even becomes accustomed to miracles. Gradually I began walking to the treatment room. By some odd quirk, the doctor prescribed this one morning. I went just as I was, barefoot, wrapped in my blanket to cover my shirt, and in the crisp air among the many familiar smells, I discovered a new fragrance: that of the blossoming spring. I was almost positive of this as I considered the passage of time. On my return I noticed in passing two men in convicts' uniforms who pulled or rather dragged a large oxcart on rubber wheels, the type that they usually attach to trucks. On it I glimpsed some frozen, dangling, yellow-looking limbs and some other chopped-up body parts. I quickly pulled the blanket tightly around my shoulders so as not to catch a cold. I tried to hop back to my warm room as soon as possible, to wipe my feet a little for the sake of decorum, and then to get under my blanket and settle in as quickly as possible. Here I conversed with my neighbor as long as he remained there (because after some time he went "back home" and an older Polish man took his place).

I looked around at everything in the scene worthy of note and listened to the orders blaring from the loudspeaker, and I must say from these bare facts—assisted, of course, by my imagination—I surmised, I conjured up a picture of the whole camp, its every color, smell, and taste, the comings and goings, its every movement, small and large events from early dawn until the late curfew and at times even later than that. The call of the barbers to the bath, "Friseure zum Bad, Friseure zum Bad," which was issued several times daily, and sometimes more often, clearly signaled that a new transport had arrived. In conjunction with this call, there was the inevitable "Leichen-kommando zum Tor!" (that is, "Corpse-carriers to the gate!"), and when they repeated that call, asking for some reserves, I could deduce the size and quality of the transport. I also learned that on these occasions the *Effekten* (that is, the "storage workers") were asked to hurry to the clothes storage facilities, sometimes even in *Laufschritt* (that is, "on the run"). If, on the other hand, they call for two or four *Leichenantragers* [body-bearers], let's say with one or two stretchers, with "Zwei Tragbetten sofort zum Tor!" [Two stretchers quickly to the gate!], then you could be sure that there had been an accident of some sort: at work, at interrogation, in the cellar, in the attic, who knows where?

I also learned that the *Kartoffelschäler* (that is, "potato-peeler squad") had not only a day shift but also a night one and many other such things. But at precisely the same time every afternoon, there was the enigmatic message: "Ela zwo, Ela zwo, aufmarschieren lassen!" and I got a headache trying to unravel this mystery. It was quite simple, though, and I finally made sense of it from the endless, churchlike silences that invariably followed that message, from both the commands "Mützen ab!" "Mützen auf!" [Caps off! Caps on!] and the occasional thin sound of music. I discovered that the camp was standing at parade out there: *aufmarschieren lassen*, therefore, referred to the order for gathering for review; *zwo* must stand for *zwei* [two]; and *ela* apparently must be *LA*, that is, *Lagerältester*, or camp commander. And so it seemed that in Buchenwald there had to be two camp commanders at work, which was really no surprise, after all, in a camp where, according to what I had heard, they had long ago passed 90,000 in assigning prisoner numbers. Gradually our room also fell silent. Zbisek had already departed if it was his turn to visit, and Pjetyka cast a final glance around before turning off the lights with his customary "good night." Then I found the most comfort my bed was able to offer and that my wounds permitted, pulled my cover over my ears, and was soon surprised by a carefree sleep. No, I couldn't have wished for more than this in a concentration camp. I couldn't have done better than this, I had to admit.

Still, two problems worried me a little. One was my wounds. Doubtless they still existed, since the surrounding area was hot and feverish and the flesh was still raw, but around the edges a thin membrane was forming, and there were signs of scabs. Now the doctor no longer stuffed them with gauze. He rarely ordered me to return for treatment, and if he did, then everything was wrapped up in a disconcertingly short time, and his face on these occasions took on a disconcertingly pleased expression. My second concern was an admittedly joyful event, which was not impossible. When Pjetyka and Zbisek, for instance, interrupted their conversation and with raised forefingers asked for silence from us, then I too could hear some distant, dull noise, at times some uninterrupted sounds reminiscent of barking dogs. Next door, too, beyond the dividing wall where I suspected Bohus's room to be, there was a lot of liveliness nowadays, as I was capable of judging from the noises filtering through, even well after lights were out. The many sounds of sirens were an everyday occurrence now, and often one was awakened at night by the loudspeaker's call, "Krematorium, ausmachen," that is, "Shut down the crematorium," and a minute later, but very annoyingly, "Krematorium! Sofort ausmachen!" From this I understood that they most assuredly didn't want the sparkles to aid the enemy airplanes in tracking them down.

I have no idea when the barbers slept. I was informed that some of the newcomers were forced to stand around naked for two to three days before being allowed to enter the baths. The corpse-carriers, too, I heard, worked ceaselessly around the clock. There was not one single empty bed in our room, and in addition to the usual abscesses, cuts, and wounds, I heard for the first time about a wound inflicted by a gun on a Hungarian boy who now occupied a bed on my other side. He had received the wound on a foot march lasting several days, coming from a provincial camp named Obadruf, if I heard him correctly, which, according to his accounts, was quite similar to Zeitz. They were marching, trying to avoid the enemy, the Americans, and the bullet was actually intended for the person next to him, who fell from the row in exhaustion, but it hit him in the leg. Fortunately, he added, the bullet hit no bones, and I thought to myself, "Well, that wouldn't have happened in my case," because in my leg, the bullet would have found some bone, regardless of where it hit, no question about that. It turned out that he had been in the camp only since fall, and his number was eighty something, not particularly outstanding or noble here in our room.

In a word, nowadays I was hearing news of impending changes, discomforts, chaos, disturbances, and trouble from everywhere. At times Pjetyka walked down the row of beds with a list in his hands asking everyone, including me: "Can you walk or run?" I told him, "Nye, nye. [No, not I] Ich kann nicht" [I cannot]. "Yes, yes," he replied, "du kannst" [you can], and with that he entered my name on the list as, incidentally, he entered everyone's, including Kuharski's, whose swollen legs were full of thousands of parallel cuts reminding one of open mouths, as I had once discovered in the treatment room. Another evening, just as I had finished chewing my bread, I heard from the loudspeaker: "Alle Juden im Lager [All Jews in the camp], sofort antreten!" (that is, "assemble at once!"), but it was spoken in such a terrifying voice that I immediately sat up in bed. "What are you doing?" Pjetyka inquired with a curious face. I pointed to the speaker, but he only smiled his usual smile and motioned with both hands: back, back, relax, what's the excitement, what's the hurry? But the loudspeaker spewed forth all evening: it was calling the club-equipped dignitaries of the camp supervisory commando to report for immediate work, and perhaps it wasn't quite satisfied with them either, because shortly thereafter—I could barely hear it without shuddering—it called for the Lagerältester and the commanding officer of the Lagerschutz. In other words, it was asking for the two highest dignitaries of the camp to come to the gate *aber im Laufschritt*, that is, "on the run!" At other times, the voice was full of questions, resentment: "Lagerältester! Aufmarschieren lassen! Lagerältester! Wo sind die Juden?" [Commanders! Have them assembled! Commanders! Where are the Jews?]. The box continued to rant and rave, to order, to call with plenty of static in between. Pjetyka simply dismissed it with a wave of his hand, annoyed. So I left the whole business up to him and lay quietly down again.

But if that evening was unpleasant, the next day they allowed no exceptions: "Lagerältester! Das ganze Lager: antreten!" [Commanders! Assemble the whole camp!]. Then shortly afterward the sounds of engines, of barking dogs, of shots from guns, and of sticks beating, the clip-clop of running feet, and the heavier sound of boots pursuing them showed (and that's what some people were hoping for) that the soldiers could take things into their own hands; and it showed what the fruit of disobedience could be. And then, finally—however it happened—there was suddenly silence.

Very soon afterward the doctor stepped in unexpectedly—since his visits usually took place in the morning—as if nothing at all were happening outside. But now he was neither cool nor collected, nor as well-groomed as usual: his face was worn, his coat was worn, his coat was stained with rust. His bloody eyes surveyed the room; obviously he was looking for an empty bed. "Wo ist der," he asked Pjetyka, "der mit dieser kleinen Wunde hier?" [Where is the one, the one with the little wound?].

With a determined gesture, he described a spot near the hip or thigh, while his inquisitive eyes rested on every face, including mine, for a second—I doubted that he failed to recognize me, even though his glance only lasted for a second—only to focus again on Pjetyka, waiting, urging, demanding an answer, making it, so to speak, Pjetyka's responsibility. I was silent, but I was beginning to get ready to get dressed to go outside into the middle of that chaos. Then, to my great surprise, I noticed that Pjetyka, at least judging by his face, had no idea to whom the doctor might be referring, and then, after some loss of time and with a sudden recognition, like someone who has just understood, he said, "Ach . . . ja" [Oh . . . yes], and pointed to the boy with the gun wound.

The doctor immediately agreed, appearing to be delighted by the choice, like a man whose problem has been guessed and finally solved by someone else. "Der geht sofort nach Hause" [He goes home at once], he ordered, and then something very strange, unusual, I'd have to say unfitting, occurred that had never been seen in our quarters until now and was impossible to witness without some sense of tension and embarrassment. The boy with the gunshot wound, after standing up, first folded his hands in front of the doctor as if preparing to pray, and then when the doctor stepped back, shocked at such impropriety, the boy fell on his knees in front of him and, grabbing his legs with both hands, locked his arms around them. Then all I saw was the quick flash of the doctor's hand, and all I heard was the sound of a smack on the boy's face, and while I understood none of the doctor's words, I sensed his outrage as he pushed this obstruction out of his way and stormed out the door, his face more crimson than usual.

A new patient was placed in the now-empty bed, again a boy, and judging from the now-familiar square of bandage on his foot, he was toeless. The next time Pjetyka approached me, I quietly spoke to him, thanking him. But from his response, "What?" to my insistent questions about what had happened *früher, vorher* (that is, "before, just before"), he replied with an expression of total lack of understanding, total ignorance, even marvel, shaking his head. From that I realized that this time it was I, it seems, who had committed an improperiety and that accordingly we had to manage certain things by ourselves. But to begin with, everything happened according to the rules of justice—that at least was my opinion—because, after all, I had lived in the room longer and also because the other boy was in a better general condition, and because, without question—at least to my mind—he stood a better chance out there, and, finally, because I was able to accept a situation more easily when it concerned someone else's bad luck rather than my own. This was the conclusion I arrived at. This was the lesson I learned, regardless of how I pondered or examined the situation. Mostly, however, I wondered what was the good of such concern when people were shooting out there?

Two days later our windows were splattered as some stray bullets entered through the opposite wall. That day was full of activity. Suspicious-looking people kept visiting Pjetyka for a word or two, and he too stepped out several times. At times he left to go somewhere for extended periods, and in the evening he returned with a longish package under his arm or rather with something rolled up in a cylinder. At first I thought that this was a sheet, but no, it couldn't be because it had a handle. Then I thought that it was a white flag, but from its center something poked out, something that I had never seen in the hands of a prisoner, and at the sight of it the whole room came into motion, hissed, murmured. It was an object that, before placing it under his bed, Pjetyka showed to everyone very quickly, but with such a smile and with such a gesture, clutching it to his breast, that I even felt almost as if I was under a Christmas tree, in the possession of a longed-for, valuable gift: it was a brown, wooden object with a bluish metal pipe sticking out of it—a sawed-off shotgun. I remembered that expression from reading my beloved cops-and-robbers novels a long time ago.

The next day, once again, promised to be busy. But who could keep count of every single day and every single event? At any rate, I can report that the kitchen continued to function smoothly, and the doctor was also almost always punctual. On a certain morning, shortly after coffee, there were hurried steps in the corridor and a loud shout, like a password, to which Pjetyka speedily responded by pulling his package out from its hiding place, grabbing it, and disappearing. Not much later, around nine, I heard soldiers, not prisoners, for the first time on the loudspeaker repeating twice in a row: "Zu allen der SS Angehörigen das Lager sofort zu verlassen" (that is, "Instructions for all the SS men to leave the camp immediately").

Then I heard the distant but approaching noise of battle, at times deafening, as if the bullets were flying around my ears, then only sporadic, and then finally everything fell silent— much too silent, because I vainly waited, listened, strained myself to hear the clashing of pots and the sound of the soup carriers.

It was probably around four in the afternoon when the loudspeaker came on again, and after some static and some sounds of someone blowing into the microphone, we were informed that the Lagerältester was speaking. "Comrades," he said in a clearly moved voice, vacillating between too sharp a pitch and choking at the onset of some emotion that was obviously suffocating him, "wir sind frei!" [We are free!], and I was thinking to myself: "Well, then, the Lagerältester must share the philosophy of Pjetyka, Bohus, the doctor, and their likes. He must have been in cahoots with them if he is the one announcing the event, and with such obvious joy." Then he gave a short, neat speech, and then others followed calling for attention in a variety of languages: in French, in Czech, and in a melodious language that recalled the pleasant memories of the people of the bath squad, which I had heard upon my arrival here. Then "Uvaga, uvaga!" [Attention, attention!]: as a response to this the Polish patient next to me immediately sat up in his bed all excited and shouted at us, "Honor from now on to the Polish Communists!" Only then did I remember how he had wiggled, writhed, and been nervous all day long. And then to my great surprise, I heard in Hungarian: "Attention, attention, this is the Hungarian camp council." I was thinking to myself:

"Well, well, well, I had no idea that there even was such a thing."

But still, I listened unhappily to all the other announcements. All I heard were speeches about freedom—not a single word, not a single reference to the missing soup. I too was very glad, of course, that we were free, even if, on the other hand, I had to admit that yesterday such a thing couldn't have happened, but we always had our soup on time then. It was already dark outside, that April evening. Pjetyka had returned, flushed, excited, bursting with a thousand words I was unable to understand, when finally the camp commander again spoke over the loudspeaker. Now he was addressing members of the former potato-peeling squad, asking them to please be kind enough to take up their former positions in the kitchen. He asked the remaining inhabitants of the camp to stay awake even until the middle of the night because they were just now beginning to prepare some good strong goulash soup for us. Only then did I fall back, relieved, onto my pillow. Only then did something relax within me, and only then did I myself begin to think seriously about freedom.

11

I came home at around the same time of year as I had left. At any rate, the forests all around Buchenwald were green, grass was already sprouting over the mass graves of buried corpses, and the recently abandoned asphalt of the mustering square was scattered with the remnants of all sorts of rags, papers, and tins, while unused fire sites were glistening in the midsummer heat. I was asked in Buchenwald if I felt like attempting the return trip. We young people were to go together under the guidance of a stocky, bespectacled man with graying hair, who was one of the officials of the Hungarian camp council. He was supposed to arrange our affairs during the trip. We'd now have the use of a truck and the cooperation of the American soldiers to drive us for a while eastward. The rest of the journey would be up to us, the man said, as he encouraged us to call him Uncle Miklós. "We'll have to get on with our lives," he added, and, indeed, I had to admit we couldn't do anything else, since we now had the opportunity. All in all I considered myself fit, aside from a few strangenesses and inconveniences. For instance, if I poked my finger into my flesh anywhere, at least for a long time, the spot and the indentation were as visible as if I had poked some lifeless, unelastic material, like cheese or wax.

My face, too, surprised me. When I first looked at it in one of the spacious rooms of the former SS hospital that was equipped with a mirror, I was surprised, because I remembered a different face from my past. What I saw was a face with a noticeably short forehead under freshly sprouting hair, strangely widening ear roots next to brand-new, awkward swellings, bags, and soft pockets in other places. All in all, judging from the testimony of my former readings, these were the facial characteristics of a man who had indulged to excess in all the pleasures of the flesh and had therefore aged prematurely. I also remembered a much more friendly, I could even say more trust-inspiring, expression in my eyes, which seemed to have become quite small. In addition, I hobbled and was dragging my right foot a little. "No matter," said Uncle Miklós. "It will be cured by the home air. At home," he announced, "we'll make a new place for ourselves," and as a beginning he taught us a few new songs. As we marched through villages or small towns, which happened occasionally, we sang songs in neat, militarylike, three-man rows. My favorite was a song beginning "At the borders of Madrid, we are manning the gates." I couldn't really tell you why. I also liked another one, particularly because of the lines "We labor all day, and we almost starve to death / but our work-seasoned hands are already grasping the gun!" For other reasons I also liked a song in which there was a line "We are the young guard of the proletariat," which we followed by the shout "Rot front" [Red front], because every time we shouted that, I noticed the slamming of a window or two, or the quick disappearance behind a gate of some German.

We traveled lightly, with the awkward, uncomfortably shaped military pack of American soldiers, which was a light-blue canvas bag that was too narrow and too long. In it I had two thick blankets, a change of underclothes, a gray, good-quality sweater with green borders that had been left in the SS storage house, and, of course, food provisions for the journey, such as cans and other things. I wore the green pants of the American army, their durable-looking, rubber-soled, laced shoes with the accompanying indestructible leather foot protector, complete with buckles and strings. For my head I found a funny-shaped cap that proved to be a little too heavy for the season, ornamented on the stiff front and the bordered top with a square, or rather a rhomboid, to use its proper geometric name. It must have belonged to some Polish officer before me, I was informed. I probably could have done better in choosing a coat from the storage, but finally I contented myself with the well-worn, familiarly striped prisoner's garment without the number and the triangle, but otherwise unchanged. In fact I chose it, I'd almost say, because I was attached to it. This way, at least, there would be no misunderstanding, I thought, and besides, I considered it a pleasant, functional, cool garment, at least now, in the summer.

We traveled by truck, by oxcart, on foot, and by public transportation—whatever the different armies were able to make available for us. We slept on oxcarts, on the abandoned benches of schoolrooms, or under the starry sky on the soft grass of parks surrounded by neat gingerbread houses. We even traveled by boat on a river called the Elbe, which to eyes accustomed to the Danube appeared to be rather small. We passed through former cities that were now nothing but places of rubble, with a few black remnants of walls in between. Around this rubble and walls and the remnants of bridges now lived and slept the original inhabitants. I tried to be glad about this, since I felt that those people had put a damper on my joy. I traveled on a red streetcar and on a real train in a real passenger car, one intended for people, even if the only place for me, at times, was on top of it.

We stopped in a city where, in addition to Czech, I also heard Hungarian spoken, and while we were waiting for the promised connection in the evening, people surrounded us outside the train station. They kept questioning us: Were we coming from a concentration camp? They also asked me if I had met a relative of theirs by such and such a name. I told them that in general people have no names in a concentration camp. Then they tried to describe these people, what they looked like, their faces, hair colors, features. I tried to make them understand: it's no good, because in a concentration camp people usually change entirely.

Then they gradually dispersed, with the exception of one man, who was dressed in a summery fashion in shirtsleeves and pants and who linked his two thumbs through his suspenders on both sides close to where they were attached to his pants and drummed with the rest of his fingers, playing with the cloth. He was curious to know—which made me smile a little—if I had seen the gas chambers. I told him that if I had, then we wouldn't be having this conversation. "Well, yes," he said, "but were there really any gas chambers?" and I answered, "Yes, of course, along with other things, they also had gas chambers. It all depends," I added, "which camp specialized in what. In Auschwitz, for instance, we could count on them. On the other hand," I said, "I'm coming from Buchenwald." "From where?" he asked, and I had to repeat, "From Buchenwald." "From Buchenwald, then," he nodded, and I said, "Yes, from there." To this he replied, "Well, let's see," with a strict, almost magisterially teaching expression on his face, "well then, you" (and he used the polite form of *you*, which made me feel quite solemn in response to his serious, and I would almost say ceremonious, address), "well then, you heard about the gas chambers." I told him, "Yes, of course, I did." "And yet," he went on, with the same stiff, stricken look on his face, as if he wanted to bring order and light into everything, "you have not convinced yourself with your own eyes." And I had to admit, "No, I haven't." "Well then," he said, and with a short nod he walked away stiffly with a straightened back, and from what I could see, he looked very satisfied about something, if I wasn't mistaken.

Very soon they called out: "Hurry, the train is in the station," and I was able to find a passable seat on the wide wooden step of the entrance to a car. I woke up in the morning hearing the cheerful puffs of the locomotive. Later my attention was riveted, because I could now read all the place-names in Hungarian. A glinting body of water that made my eyes blink was the Danube, someone told me, and this land all around it, which sweated and trembled in the morning light, was now Hungary. After a while we arrived at a station with broken windows and a worn-out roof: "The Western Train Station," people around me said, and indeed it was. Yes, I recognized it.

Out there in front of the building the sun was hitting the

sidewalk. The day was warm, noisy, dusty, and busy. The street-cars were yellow and carried the number six; this was also the same as in the past. There were merchants, too, with strange cookies, newspapers, and other goods. The people looked very beautiful and obviously were all busy, having important preoccupations. Everyone hurried, ran somewhere, pushing one another in different directions. I was told that we had to go immediately to an emergency help center to give our names, so that we could receive some money and papers, the inevitable necessities of life. This particular place was near the other train station, the Eastern, and at the first corner we got on a street-car. Even though I found the streets more worn, the rows of houses gap-toothed, and the remaining houses often shot full of holes and without windows, I still generally remembered the way and also the square where we had to get off.

We found the center opposite a movie house that I also remembered in a large, ugly, gray public building. Its court-yard, foyer, and corridors were already full of people. They were sitting, standing, moving about, making noises, chitchat-ting, or being silent. There were many who wore the eclectic, hand-me-down uniforms of various armies and storage facili-ties. Some wore striped coats like mine, but others were al-ready dressed in civilian attire, with white shirts and neckties, and with their hands linked behind their backs they were once again discussing important affairs of state, just as they had done before going to Auschwitz. Here they were recalling conditions in a certain camp, comparing one with another. They were discussing the sum and total of the assistance that we were to receive, and somewhere else they were objecting to the procedures of the administration, while others were discov-ering injustices in the payment promises. In one respect they all agreed: We'll have to wait, and we'll have to wait for a long time. This bored me, so I threw my sack over my shoulders and walked back to the courtyard, where I left through the gate to the outside. I saw the movie theater again and remembered that on my right, one or two blocks further down, if I wasn't mistaken, Nefelejcs Street would cross my path.

I found the house easily. It was still standing and was in no way different from the other yellow or gray, somewhat tattered buildings on the street. At least that was my impression. In the cool gateway I saw in the old, worn, earmarked register of names that the number was also correct, and that I had to climb up to the second floor. Slowly, I held on and climbed the steps of the somewhat rotten and sour-smelling staircase, from whose windows I could see the circular corridors and the sadly clean courtyard with a little grass in its middle, and of course the usual sad tree trying to survive with its half-bare, dusty leaves. Across the court a woman with a scarf over her hair hurried to shake out her dust rag. From somewhere the music from a radio reached my ears. Somewhere a child cried, furiously.

When the door finally opened in front of me, I was surprised, because after such a long time I suddenly saw Bandi Citrom's small slit black eyes in front of me again, only this time in the face of a youngish, black-haired, stocky, not very tall woman. She stepped back a little, probably, I thought, because of my coat, and in order to prevent her from slamming the door in my face, I asked: "Is Bandi Citrom home?" "No," she answered. I asked, "Is he back now or not?" She shook her head and closed her eyes and answered, "Not yet." Only when she opened her eyes again did I notice that her lower eyelashes were shining from some moisture. Her mouth contracted a little too, and then I thought I should leave right away, but from the foyer a thin, black-scarfed old woman emerged, and I told her too that I was looking for Bandi Citrom. She also said, "He's not home." She added this, however: "Come back some other time. Maybe in a few days." And I noticed that the younger woman turned her head in response to this with a strange, rejecting gesture, but at the same time powerlessly, helplessly. She also lifted the outer portion of her hand to her lips as if trying to suffocate a word, a sound that wanted to escape.

Then I felt compelled to explain to the old woman: "We were together in Zeitz." She asked, in a severe tone, almost calling me to account: "Then why didn't you come home together?" I almost had to apologize: "Because we were separated. I was sent somewhere else." Then she wanted to know, "Are there still Hungarians up there?" "Of course, a lot," I answered. In reply to this she turned triumphantly to the young woman: "You see!" Then she said to me: "I've been saying they're only now starting to come home. But my daughter is impatient. She doesn't want to believe anything anymore." I almost felt that in my view her daughter was right, that she was the one who knew Bandi Citrom better. Then the old woman said: "Come on in," but I told her that I had to go home first. "Your parents must be waiting for you," she said, and I answered, "Yes, of course." "Well, then," she added, "hurry home so you can make them happy." And with that I left.

On reaching the train station, I climbed aboard a streetcar because my leg was hurting and because I recognized one out of many with a familiar number. A thin old woman wearing a strange, old-fashioned lace collar moved away from me. Soon a man came by with a hat and a uniform and asked to see my ticket. I told him I had none. He insisted that I should buy one. I said I had just come back from abroad and was penniless. He looked at my coat, then at me, then at the old woman, and then he informed me that there were rules governing public transportation that not he but people above him had made. He said that if I didn't buy a ticket, I'd have to get off. I told him my leg ached, and I noticed that the old woman responded to this by turning to look outside the window, in an insulted way, as if I were somehow accusing her of who knows what. Then through the car's open door a large, black-haired man noisily galloped in. He wore a shirt without a tie and a light canvas suit. From his shoulder a black box hung, and an attaché case was in his hand. "What a shame!" he shouted. "Give him a ticket," he ordered, and he gave or rather pushed a coin toward the conductor. I tried to thank him, but he interrupted me, looking around, annoyed: "Some people ought to be ashamed of themselves!" he said, but the conductor was already gone. The old woman continued to stare outside.

179

Then with a softened voice he said to me: "Are you coming from Germany, son?" "Yes," I said. "From a concentration camp?" "Yes, of course." "Which one?" "Buchenwald." "Yes," he answered, he had heard of it—one of the "pits of Nazi hell." "Where did they carry you away from?" "Budapest." "How long were you there?" "One year." "You must have seen a lot, son, a lot of terrible things," he said, but I didn't reply. "Anyway," he went on, "what's important is that it's over, it's finished," and with a cheerful face pointing to the buildings that we were passing, he asked me to tell him what I now felt, being home again, seeing the city I had left. I answered, "Hatred." He fell silent, but soon he observed that, unfortunately, he had to say that he understood how I felt. He also felt that "under certain circumstances" there is a place and a role for hatred, "even a benefit," and, he added, he assumed that we understood each other, and he knew full well the people I hated. I told him, "Everyone." Then he fell silent again, this time for a longer period, and then he asked: "Did you have to go through many horrors?" I answered, "That depends on what you call a horror." Surely, he replied with a tense face, I had been deprived of a lot, had gone hungry, and had probably been beaten. I said, "Naturally." "Why do you keep saying 'naturally,' son," he exclaimed, seeming to lose his temper, "when you are referring to things that are not natural at all?" "In a concentration camp," I said, "they are very natural." "Yes, yes," he gasped, "it's true there, but . . . well . . . but the concentration camp itself is not natural." He seemed to have found the appropriate expression, but I didn't even answer him, because I began to understand that there are certain subjects you can't discuss, it seems, with strangers, ignorant people, and children, one might say. Besides—I suddenly noticed an unchanged, only slightly more bare and uncared-for square—it was time for me to get off, and I told him so. But he came after me, and pointing to a backless bench over in the shade, he suggested, "Let's sit down for a minute."

First he seemed somewhat insecure. "To tell the truth," he observed, "it's only now that the horrors are beginning to surface, and the world is still standing speechless and without understanding before the question How could all this have happened?" I was quiet, but he turned toward me and said: "Son, wouldn't you like to tell me about your experiences?" I was a little surprised and told him that I couldn't tell him very many interesting things. Then he smiled a little and said, "Not to me, to the world." Even more astonished, I replied, "What should I talk about?" "The hell of the camps," he replied, but I answered that I couldn't say anything about that because I didn't know anything about hell and couldn't even imagine what it was like. He assured me that this was simply a metaphor. "Shouldn't we picture the concentration camp like hell?" he asked. I answered, while drawing circles in the dust with my heels, that people were free to ignore it according to their means and pleasure but that, as far as I was concerned, I was only able to picture the concentration camp because I knew it a bit, but I didn't know hell at all. "But, still, if you tried," he insisted. After a few more circles, I answered, "In that case I'd imagine it as a place where you can't be bored. But," I added, "you can be bored in a concentration camp, even in Auschwitz—given, of course, certain circumstances." Then he fell silent and asked, almost as if it was against his will: "How do you explain that?" After giving it some thought, I said, "By the time." "What do you mean 'by the time'?" "Because time helps." "Helps? How?" "It helps in every way."

I tried to explain how fundamentally different it is, for instance, to be arriving at a station that is spectacularly white, clean, and neat, where everything becomes clear only gradually, step by step, on schedule. As we pass one step, and as we recognize it as being behind us, the next one already rises up before us. By the time we learn everything, we slowly come to understand it. And while you come to understand everything gradually, you don't remain idle at any moment: you are already attending to your new business; you live, you act, you move, you fulfill the new requirements of every new step of development. If, on the other hand, there were no schedule, no gradual enlightenment, if all the knowledge descended on you at once right there in one spot, then it's possible neither your brains nor your heart could bear it. I tried to explain this to him as he fished out a torn package from his pocket and offered me a wrinkled cigarette, which I declined. Then, after two large inhalations, supporting his elbows on his knees with his upper body leaning forward, he said, without looking at me, in a colorless, dull voice: "I understand."

"On the other hand," I continued, "there is the unfortunate disadvantage that you somehow have to pass away the time. I've seen prisoners who were there for 4, 6, or even 12 years or more who were still hanging on in the camp. And these people had to spend these 4, 6, or 12 years times 365 days—that is, 12 times 365 times 24 hours—in other words, they had to somehow occupy the time by the second, the minute, the day. But then again," I added, "that may have been precisely what helped them too, because if the whole time period had descended on them in one fell swoop, they probably wouldn't have been able to bear it, either physically or mentally, the way they did." Because he was silent, I added: "You have to imagine it this way." He answered the same as before, except now he covered his face with his hands, threw the cigarette away, and then said in a somewhat more subdued, duller voice: "No, you can't imagine it." I, for my part, thought to myself: "That's probably why they say 'hell' instead."

Then he straightened himself up and glanced at his watch, and the expression on his face changed completely. He informed me that he was a reporter, "for a democratic paper," and then I realized that some of his words had vaguely reminded me of Uncle Vili's, as well as the words and deeds and the stubbornness of the rabbi and Uncle Lajos. This idea made me aware now for the first time of the genuine prospect of a soon-to-occur reunion, and so I was only halfway attentive to him. He'd like, he said, to turn our chance encounter into a lucky event and suggested, "Let's write an article together. Let's start a series of articles." He would write the articles, but based entirely on my words. In this way, I could get my hands on some money, which I most probably could use at the onset of my "new life," even though, he added with a somewhat apologetic smile, he couldn't offer very much because his paper was new and its "financial resources modest." But at this moment for him "the healing of the still-bleeding wounds and the punishment of the guilty" were the most important considerations, he said. "But, above all, one has to mobilize public opinion," eliminate "indifference, or even doubt." Traditionalists were of no use here whatsoever. In his opinion there was a need to expose reason, the truth, regardless of "how painful a tribulation" we'd have to face. He saw a lot of originality in my words, and in them the revelation of our time in its totality, if I understood him correctly. He heard the "sad stamp" of our time in my talk, which gave "a new, individual color to the wearisome flood of facts." After this, he asked for my opinion.

I explained that I had to take care of my own business first. But he misunderstood me, it seems, because he said: "No. This is no longer just *your* business. It's ours, all of ours, the whole world's." I told him yes, but it was still time for me to go home. Then he apologized. We stood up, but he seemed hesitant, seemed to ponder something. Couldn't we begin the article, he wondered, with a picture of the moment of reunion? I didn't answer, and then, with a tiny half smile, he remarked that "a reporter is sometimes forced to commit insensitivities because of his profession," and if I didn't feel like it, he didn't want to insist. Then he sat down, opened a black notebook on his lap, jotted something down quickly, tore out the page, and, standing up again, handed me the paper. It contained his name and the address of his press. He then said good-bye, "hope to see you again soon." Then I felt the friendly pressure of his warm, meaty, somewhat sweaty hand. I had found the conversation with him pleasant and relaxing, and he was likable and well intentioned. I waited until his figure disappeared in the bustle of the crowd, and only then did I toss away the piece of paper.

A few steps further along the way, I recognized our building. It still stood, in its entirety, in good shape. Inside the gate was the old smell. The shaky lift with its barred enclosure and the yellow, worn steps greeted me. Further up I was able to say hello to a familiar turn of the staircase in a particularly memorable moment. On reaching our floor, I rang the doorbell. It opened quickly but only exposed a chink, stopped by a chain lock. That surprised me, because I didn't recall such a contraption from the past. A strange face appeared in the door's chink: the yellow, bony face of a woman about middle age peered out at me. She asked me whom I was looking for, and I answered, "I live here." "No," she answered, "we live here." She was about to shut the door, but she couldn't because I held it open with my foot. I tried to explain to her: "There must be some mistake, because I left from here, and most certainly we *do* live here." She, on the other hand, kept insisting that it was I who was mistaken, because without doubt *they* lived there, and with a cordial, polite, and sympathetic shaking of her head, she tried to close the door, while I tried to prevent this. For a second, though, I looked up at the number to be sure that I hadn't perhaps made a mistake, and my foot must have slipped then, because her attempt proved successful, and she slammed the door shut and turned the key twice.

Returning to the staircase, I was stopped by another familiar door. I rang the bell. A fat, fleshy female appeared. She was going to shut the door too—I was beginning to get used to such treatment—but a pair of glasses glistened, and Uncle Fleischmann's gray face appeared in the semidark. Next to him was a weighty belly, slippers, a large red beard, a childish hairdo, the dead remnant of a cigar: old Mr. Steiner revealed himself precisely as I had left him on the last night before the day at the customhouse. They stood staring at me, then called out my name, and old Mr. Steiner gave me a hug just as I was, in my hat, striped prisoner's coat, and all sweaty. They ushered me into the living room, and Aunt Fleischmann hurried into the kitchen to rustle up "a bite to eat," as she put it. I had to answer the usual questions: From where, how, when? Then I asked and heard that, indeed, other people were now living in our apartment. I asked, "And us?"

Because they seemed to be having a hard time getting started, I asked, "And my father?" As a response, they fell completely silent. After a little while a hand—I believe it was Uncle Steiner's—slowly rose and descended like a careful old bat on my arm. Of what they told me then, I basically recall that "the validity of the sad news, unfortunately, cannot be doubted," because it is based "on the testimony of former co-inmates," according to whom my father died "after a short period of suffering" in a German camp, which, however, lies in Austrian territory. What was the name of the camp? Mant-hausen? No, Mauthausen. They rejoiced at remembering it and then turned serious again. Yes, that's how it was.

I asked about my mother: Did they happen to have any news of her? They let me know right away that yes, indeed, they had some good news: she was alive, she was healthy, she had been here in the house a few months ago asking about me. They had seen her themselves and had spoken with her. "And my step-mother?" I asked, and I found out: "Well, in the meantime she remarried." Who? I wanted to know, and again they got a little tied up on the name. One said, "Kovacs, I think"; the other said, "No, not Kovacs. It's Futo. I mean Suto." Then they nodded happily. Yes, of course, that's what it was: Suto, just like before. She had a lot to thank him for, "actually every-thing," they told me. Suto was the one who "saved the family fortune." He hid her "during the most difficult times." That is how they put it. "But maybe," Uncle Fleischmann mused, "she was a little too quick," and old Mr. Steiner agreed. "But in the last analysis," Mr. Steiner added, "it was understandable," and the other old man agreed.

I stayed with them for a while because some time had passed since I had sat down this way in a wine-colored, soft, uphol-stered armchair. Meanwhile, Aunt Fleischmann returned and brought me some bread with lard, paprika, and some thin slices of onions on an ornately bordered white china plate. She said she remembered that this food had pleased me, and I quickly reassured her that this was still true. As I ate, the two old men told me, "Well, life wasn't easy at home either." From the whole account I only caught a misty sketch of some confus-ing, disturbing events that, essentially, I could neither picture nor understand. Instead, I noticed the frequent, almost tiredly repeated recurrence of a single phrase in their speeches with which they designated every new turn of events and change: for example, the yellow stars "came about," October 15 "came about," the Arrow "came about," the ghetto "came about," the Danube event "came about," liberation "came about."

And then, I also noticed a recurring mistake: it was as if all these fading, rather unimaginable, barely reconstructible events hadn't taken place in the normal confines of minutes, hours, days, weeks, and months, but, so to speak, all at once, somehow in a single swirl of dizzy chaos, as if they had happened at a strange afternoon gathering that had turned unexpectedly sour when the many participants—God knows how—suddenly lost their heads and finally didn't even know what they were doing. At a certain moment they both fell silent, and after some moments of quiet old Mr. Fleischmann suddenly asked me: "What are your plans for the future?" I was a little surprised and told him that I hadn't given it much thought. Then the other old man stirred and bent toward me in his chair. The bat also rose again and alighted, this time not on my arm but on my knee. "Above all," he said, "you must forget the terrors." I asked, even more surprised, "Why?" "So that you may live." And Uncle Fleischmann nodded in agreement, adding "to live freely." To this the other nodded and said: "With such a burden one can't start a new life." He did have something of a point there, I have to admit.

Only I didn't quite understand how they could hope for something that was impossible, and I said that what had happened had indeed happened, and after all, I couldn't command my memory to follow orders. I could only start a new life, I said, if I were born again or if some disease or accident affected my brain, which I hoped they didn't wish upon me. Besides, I added, I couldn't remember seeing any horrors. Then I noticed that they were surprised. How were they to take that remark: "couldn't remember seeing"? Then I asked them in turn what they had been doing during those "difficult times." "Well, we lived," one old man mused. "We tried to survive it," added the

186

other. That means, I said, that they too kept taking one step after another. What was that supposed to mean? they wanted to know. And then I told them how that worked, for example, in Auschwitz. You had to count on about three thousand people per train—maybe not always and maybe not exactly, because I don't know for sure—but at least that's how many there were in my case. Let's just take the men; that makes about one thousand. Let's count on one to two seconds for the examination, one usually more than two. Let's not consider the first and the last, because they don't even count. But in the middle, where I was waiting, we were forced to wait ten to twenty minutes until we reached the decision station: Were we gassed right now, or were we given a momentary reprieve? During all this time the rows kept moving, kept progressing. Everybody was taking a step forward, smaller or larger depending on the speed of the operation.

Then there was silence, interrupted by only the noise of Mrs. Fleischmann taking the empty plate from in front of me and carrying it away. I didn't see her return. The two old men asked, "Where does all this fit in, and what do you mean to say by it?" I answered, "Nothing in particular. Only saying that it all 'came to pass' isn't entirely accurate," because we did it step by step. It was only now that everything looked so finished, unalterable, final, so incredibly fast, and so terribly hazy, so that it seems to have simply come to pass—only now, retroactively, as we look at it backward. Of course if we had known our fates ahead of time, then, indeed, all we could have done was to keep track of the passing of time. A silly kiss, then, is just as inevitable, for instance, as a day without activity at the customhouse or at the gas chamber. But whether we look forward or backward, we are in either case moving, I said. Because, in fact, twenty minutes is in principle a rather long stretch of time. Each minute started, lasted, and then ended before the next one started up again.

Then I asked them to consider: "Every single minute could have actually brought about a new state of affairs." It didn't, naturally, but one has to admit that it could have. In the final analysis, something might have happened during one of them, something other than what was actually happening in Auschwitz as well as here at home, let's say, as we were saying good-bye to my father.

At my last words old Mr. Steiner started moving around. "But what were we to do?" he asked, half annoyed, half complaining. I told him, "Nothing, naturally—or," I added, "anything, which would have been just as senseless as our not having done anything at all, naturally. But that is not the point," I tried to explain. "Then what is it?" they asked, since they were also beginning to lose their patience, as I was feeling progressively angry myself. "The point is in the steps. Everyone stepped forward as long as he could: I, too, took my steps—not only in the row in Auschwitz but before at home. I stepped forward with my father, with my mother, with Anne-Marie, and—maybe the most difficult step of all—with the older sister. Now I could tell her what it means to be 'a Jew': it had meant nothing for me until the steps began. Now there is no other blood, and there is nothing but"—here I got stuck, but then I remembered the words of the newspaper man—"but given situations and concomitant givens within them."

I, too, had lived out a given fate. It wasn't my fate, but I am the one who lived it to the end. I simply couldn't understand why I couldn't get this through their heads: now I will have to go somewhere and do something; now I can't content myself with assuming that it was all a mistake, an aberration, some sort of an accident or that, in some way, it never really happened. I could see, I could see clearly that they didn't understand me and that my words were not to their liking, that some even annoyed them outright. I noticed that Uncle Steiner occasionally wanted to interrupt. He wanted to jump up, and I also noticed that the other old man held him back, and I heard him say: "Let him be. Don't you see he just wants to talk? Let him speak, let him."

And I did talk, possibly in vain and possibly a little incomprehensibly. Still, I did try to get myself across to them: "We can never start a new life. We can only continue the old one. I took my own steps. No one else did. And I remained honest in the end to my given fate. The only stain or beauty flaw, I might say the only incorrectness, that anyone could accuse me of is maybe the fact that we are talking now. But that is not my doing. Do you want all this horror and all my previous steps to lose their meaning entirely? Why this sudden turn, why this opposition? Why can't you see that if there is such a thing as fate, then there is no freedom? If, on the other hand," I continued, more and more surprised at myself and more and more wound up, "if, on the other hand, there is freedom, then there is no fate. That is," and I stopped to take a breath, "that is, we ourselves are fate." I recognized this all of a sudden and with such clarity that I had never seen before. I was a little sorry that I was only facing them and not someone more intelligent—let's say, more worthy opponents. But they were the ones who were here, at that moment, and at any rate they were the ones who had also been there when we were saying good-bye to my father.

They too had taken their steps. They too knew. They too had seen ahead. They too had said good-bye to my father as if we were already hurrying out. Later, all they fought about was whether I should take the local tram or the local bus on the way to Auschwitz. At this point not only Uncle Steiner but also Uncle Fleischmann jumped up. He tried to restrain Uncle Steiner but was no longer able. "What?" he screamed at me, his face crimson-red and his fist beating against his chest. "What? Are *we* now the guilty ones—we, the victims?" I tried to explain to him: "It's not that this is a sin. We ought to simply, modestly recognize it for the sake of our honor, so to speak." They had to try to understand that they couldn't take everything away from me. It couldn't be that I was either the victim or the vanquished, that I couldn't be right and that I couldn't have been mistaken, that I was not the reason or the result of anything. I almost begged them to understand this. I couldn't simply swallow this silly bitterness simply for the sake of becoming innocent again. Still, I saw that they didn't want to understand anything, and so I took my cap and my bag and left in the middle of a few confused words, in another unfinished sentence.

Downstairs the street received me. I'd have to take a streetcar to go to see my mother. But then I remembered. Of course, I had no money, so I decided to walk. In order to gain some strength, I stopped to rest for a moment in the old square on the same bench as before. There, ahead, in the direction I'd have to go and where the street appeared to expand, lengthen, and get lost in infinity, the bluish hills were crowned by lilac clouds, and the sky was beginning to blush lilac. Around me, too, it seemed as if something had changed: there was less traffic, people's steps were slower, their voices were lower, the expressions on their faces softer. It was as if their faces were turning to one another. It was that special hour—I recognized it now, I recognized it here—my favorite hour in the camp, and a sharp, painful, futile desire grasped my heart: homesickness. All of a sudden everything came alive, everything came back, everything flooded my consciousness. I was surprised by strange moods, trembled at small memories. Yes, indeed, in a certain sense, life was purer, simpler back there. I remembered everything and everyone, even those who didn't interest me, but especially those whose existence I could validate by my presence here: Pjetyka, Bohus, the doctor, and all the rest of them. And for the first time I now thought of them with a tiny, affectionate resentment.

Let's not exaggerate things, for this is precisely the hurdle: I am here, and I know full well that I have to accept the prize of being allowed to live. Yes, as I look around me in this gentle dusk in this square on a storm-beaten yet full-of-thousands-of-promises street, I already begin to feel how readiness is growing, collecting inside me. I have to continue my uncontinuable life. My mother is waiting for me. She'll certainly be happy to see me, the poor dear. I recall how once she planned for me to become an engineer or a doctor or something like that. This is certainly what she wants. There is no impossibility that cannot be overcome (survived?), naturally, and further down the road, I now know, happiness lies in wait for me like an inevitable trap. Even back there, in the shadow of the chimneys, in the breaks between pain, there was something resembling happiness. Everybody will ask me about the deprivations, the "terrors of the camps," but for me, the happiness there will always be the most memorable experience, perhaps. Yes, that's what I'll tell them the next time they ask me: about the happiness in those camps.

If they ever do ask.

And if I don't forget.